# BORN OF THE GRAVE

## Danny Cantrell

Cover illustration by Shaun Brown

Published by Lofty Ideals, Ink

Culloden, WV

# DEDICATION

To my grandchildren, all of whom are masters of bringing light from darkness.

DANNY CANTRELL

# PROLOGUE

Steve Smith found himself in his future body again. It began as it always had; first, he was aware of his larger stature, the tall, powerful frame, a massive chest rising above a narrow waist and tight stomach muscles. I am twenty-two, he thought. Then, his eyes would open. He would emerge from total darkness and experience a brief adventure.

His favorite outings involved flying. The key, he surmised, was something inside the muscular chest, some wonderful something which allowed his body to defy gravity and lift him high above the tree tops. All he had to do was run forward with his chest expanded, and suddenly, his body levitated into the air, and he was flying, without further effort, like a bird.

On one occasion, the apple trees were in bloom, and he flew in circles around them, breathing deeply of the sweet fragrance. The carefree joy of that moment would linger for a lifetime—

But this time, things were different. Even before he opened his eyes, he knew something was wrong. The air was cool and damp, and a strong breeze blew against his face. He opened his eyes, only to find more darkness, broken by a narrow beam of light shining on a black wall. The light moved as he turned his head. A miner's lamp. He was wearing a miner's cap, like the one his father wore home from work each evening.

He had never been inside a coal mine, but now, inexplicably, that was where he was.

The mountain suddenly groaned. The shale roof over his head started cracking, and huge chunks of rock rained onto the mine floor. The earth shook, and a black cloud rushed toward him, then filled his eyes and nostrils.

He gasped for breath. His lamp was extinguished, and the world went black . . .

Seven-year-old Steve awoke in the early morning darkness, crying as he struggled to free himself from twisted, sweat soaked sheets.

He would grow to age twenty-two and beyond, but after that morning, he never dreamed again of his future self. The idealized, majestic being had perished in the mine, and Steve resigned himself to the earthbound realities of the waking world.

# CHAPTER 1

5:30 A.M.

A mud-splattered Jeep Cherokee pulled off onto a gravel driveway behind a black and white police cruiser. The driver tapped his horn twice, then turned off the ignition, leaned back in his seat, and pulled a baseball cap over his eyes.

Ten minutes later, the porch light came on, followed by a tall man with a fishing rod and tackle box in one hand and a 357 revolver in the other.

"Morning, Steve."

Steve rolled his window down. "Hey, Mike. Ready to go fishin'?"

Mike put the gun and fishing tackle on the hood of the cruiser. "Let me lock this gun in the glove box and we're on our way."

"Have any trouble getting off work today?"

"Nah. The mayor's good about letting me off."

"How about Sandy?" Steve backed out of the driveway. "She give you any grief?"

"Not lately. She used to put me in the doghouse for a week after one of these trips, but now that we've got the kids to entertain her, she don't seem to mind."

"Glad to hear it. Did you happen to see the meteor shower last night?"

"Didn't know there was one. I fell asleep on the couch watching TV."

"You missed a good show. One meteorite lit up the whole sky and broke the sound barrier. Bound to have crashed around here somewhere."

"They'll never find it in these mountains, unless it fell in one of your mine pits." Mike pulled a pastry from his tackle box and peeled off the plastic wrap. "How are things at the mine?"

"We're into the high coal now. Gonna tear the top off Bearwallow Mountain before we're through. There'll be enough level land to build a whole town up there."

"Speaking of town, how's your big brother doing in DC?"

"Alan's fine. Last I saw him was when he came back for his twentieth high school reunion last summer."

"Ours is coming up next year. Fifteen years. Can you believe it?"

"Don't remind me. We're getting to be old men."

"A single guy like you has nothing to complain about. Try living with a wife and three little kids if you want to feel your age."

"You don't have it so rough."

"I know I'm a lucky guy, but it's fun to remember the old days, when we didn't have a care in the world. Remember how the three of us used to carry our gear on our bikes and camp out down at the lake? I wish Alan could be with us today."

"Don't guess we'll be seeing those days again. The FBI does all Alan's planning for him. I'm lucky to see him once a year."

"Bet he could tell me some fine tales about the federal brand of law enforcement . . ."

"He won't talk about what he does, except to say that it takes him all over the world. Mike, you ever regret staying around here?"

"I don't have time to think about it much."

"I used to think I'd be something more. Travel the world. Invent something important. Cure a disease. Hell, I don't know. Just thought my life would be different."

"You're doing all right for yourself. Sounds like you're just getting tired of the bachelor's life." Mike washed his snack down with a big gulp of soda.

"Them's fighting words," Steve said.

"There's something to be said for stability. Granted, Alan lives in a lot bigger world than we do. But the guy couldn't settle down if he wanted to. He's married to his job and probably likes it that way."

"That he does," Steve said. "For today, I'm happy to be right here." He took one hand off the wheel and pointed toward Adkins Gas Mart. "Need anything?"

"Keep driving. I got another coke-cola and a can of worms in my tackle box. What more can a man need?"

"Just a bunch of hungry fish, old buddy, and a spit to roast them over . . ."

# CHAPTER 2

May 15, the following year.

Mike's police cruiser slid to a halt in front of the Chicago Pneumatic drill rig, raising a bigger cloud of dust than that coming from the core drilling. Steve, the superintendent for the strip mining operation, stood beside the drill operator checking his log. One hundred feet had been drilled since morning, with at least another fifty to go to reach the coal seam. He handed the log back to the operator and shouted to Mike over the noisy drilling, "Where's the fire?"

Mike kept his window up to avoid the dust, and motioned for Steve to join him in the front passenger seat.

"How about taking a ride with me, Steve?"

"Sure. Where to?"

"The cemetery over on the state line, the one you guys stripped next to a few years ago."

"The Vance cemetery? What's happening over there?"

"I got a call from Josh Vance early this morning. He was raising hell about somebody drilling into his grandfather's grave."

"Drilling into a grave? What would we be doing in a graveyard? We stripped all the coal out of there, except for what was under the cemetery. The company hasn't had any business over there since the state released the site's revegetation bond."

"I don't have any more details. I tried to calm him down, told him we'd get on it right away. Your company doesn't want any of those Vances mad at you."

"You don't have to tell me; we both went to school with them, remember?"

After a ten minute drive over a winding, single lane asphalt road, the cruiser arrived at the entrance gate to the reclaimed mine site. Steve got out of the car and unlocked the pipe gate. He motioned for Mike to drive through, then locked the gate behind them.

"These look like fresh tracks in front of us," Mike said.

"Yeah. The Vances have a key to the gate. I'll bet they're waiting at the top."

"Didn't old man Sam Vance die about a year ago?"

"Seems like. He must have been what, ninety?"

"Thereabouts."

"His grandson, Josh, worked in our underground mines for twenty years or longer. He got hurt in a rock fall eight or ten years back. Been disabled ever since."

"Another reason he's not too happy with Black Diamond Coal these days," Mike said.

After ten minutes on the winding gravel road, they reached the mountaintop, and Mike felt he had entered a different world. Gone were the rugged, steep mountains, replaced with a wide, open plateau. The strip mining operations had filled in the hollows between two once opposing ridges. The site, level for nearly a half-mile to either side, stretched ahead for three-quarters of a mile. At the far end of the reclaimed operation stood the only reminder of the former topography.

A small, round island of trees, rising two hundred feet above the plateau, was all that remained of the mountain's ridgetop. A wide ramp of earth formed a bridge from the man-made plain to the tree line.

"The cemetery's inside those trees on the knob," Steve said. "Feel free to open her up; the road's smooth up here."

Mike pushed down the accelerator, and was amazed at the ride as the speedometer hit fifty-five.

"This is better than the main highway through town."

"Thanks. This was my first project for the company. Too bad we can't afford to move the entire town up here."

When they arrived at the ramp, Steve cautioned him to slow to a crawl. "There may be some deep gullies up there. They probably used a four wheel-drive to get old man Vance's casket up the hill."

Mike soon found it impossible to navigate the cruiser through the deep ruts, so they parked the car about a third of the way up the ramp and hiked the short distance to the summit.

From the top of the ramp, they could see the cemetery, situated in a clearing in the center of the thicket of trees. A white Chevy Blazer was parked at the edge of a white picket fence that encircled the small lot. Two men, one in his mid-twenties, and another in his late forties, leaned against the vehicle.

"Howdy, Josh," Mike extended his hand to the older man. Josh hesitated, then limply shook the sheriff's hand.

"This is Steve Smith, superintendent for Black Diamond Coal's surface mining operations."

Steve offered his hand, but the man ignored the gesture.

"I heard tell of him. My boy here, Kenneth, knows him."

The younger man nodded in Steve's direction.

"That's right," Steve said. "How you doing, Ken?"

"I'm doing." The man turned his head and spat a gob of tobacco juice.

Mike could feel the hostility directed toward Black Diamond and its representative. "Show me what you've found up here."

Josh limped over to the wooden gate and opened it. The three men followed him to a granite headstone marked with the name Samuel Vance.

"This here's my granddaddy's grave," he said to Mike, ignoring Steve. "Look what they've done to it."

Josh pointed to the rounded grave mound, but nothing was apparent until Steve and Mike moved closer and looked down onto the mound.

A perfectly round hole, approximately twelve inches across, cut into the center of the mound. Mike removed a flashlight from his belt and shined it into the hole. The sides were smooth through about four feet of earth. The hole continued through the concrete vault and the metal casket lid. Mike saw the coffin's red velvet lining at the bottom—but no trace of a body, or even a clump of dirt from the mound. It was as if the body and all evidence of the digging had been vacuumed from the earth.

Mike and Steve stepped back from the grave, both amazed by what they had seen.

Josh poked Steve on the shoulder as if to challenge him to a fight.

"You tell me what you did with my granddaddy's body," Josh said.

"Mr. Vance, I don't have the slightest notion what has happened here. I've never seen anything like this."

"Look here, boy. I ain't no fool. I worked for your damned company for more than twenty years. I know what a drill hole looks like when I see one."

"Let's try to discuss this calmly, Mr. Vance." Mike placed himself between Steve and Josh. "When do you think this happened?"

"It must have been in the last two weeks," Kenneth said. "I come up here to cut brush. Decoration Day is just two weeks away. Don't guess we can have it now."

"Granddaddy was a preacher," Josh said. "Did you know that, Sheriff Stollard? Grandma is eighty-five. We might as well start digging her grave today if we have to tell her what happened to him. God'll make you pay for this." Josh pointed at Steve. "You and that company will pay, in this life or the next."

Steve kept his composure and turned to the sheriff. "You remember that big rain we had night before last, Mike? Must have been two inches. You see any water down in that hole?"

"No, not a drop."

"Neither did I," Steve said. "That must mean this happened in the last day and a half, after the big rain. Mr. Vance, do you see any tracks big enough for a Chicago Pneumatic drill? Those rigs weigh tons, yet there's no sign of any tracks coming up the ramp or next to the fence. This hole must be twelve inches across. Do you know of anything a man could carry in here and dig a hole that big?"

"Well—no," Josh said.

"I promise you, Mr. Vance, that Black Diamond had nothing to do with this," Steve said.

"Then who in God's name did?"

"That's what we mean to find out, Mr. Vance," Mike said. "Promise me you won't tell another soul. My office will do everything it can to solve this."

"Like I said, this'll kill grandma if she hears about it. We'll keep this to ourselves. Ken, get out the shovel. We've got to fill that hole before she comes up here to decorate the grave."

While Josh and Ken repaired the grave's surface damage, Steve and Mike slipped away and headed into the trees.

"What do you do from here?" Steve said.

"Walk around the clearing with me. Let's look for footprints, bent tree limbs, cigarette butts, gum wrappers—hell, I don't know, to tell you the truth."

A few minutes into the search, they heard Josh's vehicle drive off down the mountain. An hour of searching around the clearing yielded nothing more than sun-bleached candy wrappers from last year's dinner-on-the-ground held during the annual grave decoration.

# CHAPTER 3

Rose Vance sat in a cane back chair on the lawn behind her wood frame house. The years had dimmed her vision, but her sense of smell was still strong. The air was filled with the sweet smell of honeysuckle blossoms—once her favorite fragrance, but now a sad reminder of loss.

"What's the matter, Grandma?" Josh said from the chair next to her.

"This time of year brings back memories. I lost Tom, my first born, in a mining accident nearly forty years ago this month. And it's been a year since your grandpa passed on. Samuel gave me a good life, six children and all you grandkids." She lovingly squeezed Josh's hand.

"It wasn't easy, but the good Lord never promised us it would be. When we moved here, those fields were covered with trees and rocks, but we managed to scratch out a living." She gazed out into the small garden that Josh and his son, Kenneth, had planted for her at the edge of the large field.

"Preachers didn't make much in those days, but we did all right," she said. "Some folks gave donations; those that couldn't gave vegetables, fresh fruit, eggs—sometimes your grandpa would walk home with a live chicken under his arm.

"I'll be eighty-five if I make it to my next birthday. I've outlived my husband and four of my six kids. Now, I'm not long for this old world."

"Don't talk like that Grandma. You may live to see a hundred."

"I don't need to be no hundred. There's a better world waiting, and Samuel is going to be there to greet me."

She often took comfort in the words of the young minister who had officiated at her beloved's grave side, "and the dead in Christ shall rise." She knew this would be so, as surely as day follows night, but first she would go to join her Samuel. Together, she knew, they would arise, side by side, when Jesus called.

"It's time you got on home to your wife and children, Josh."

"You call me if you need anything." He bent down and kissed Rose on the forehead.

"I'll do that."

When evening came, Rose was still sitting in her favorite chair in the backyard, admiring the glow of the setting sun on the roses she planned to pick to decorate his grave.

Lost in thoughts of earlier, happier times, she paid no attention when the sun sank behind the forest at the edge of the yard. The blue sky faded to black, and the first star appeared on the horizon. The evening air chilled her bare arms and roused her from her reverie.

She arose from her chair and rubbed some warmth into her limbs. The full moon emerged over the treetops; she was reminded of the countless times she and Samuel had stood on this same spot. "Even on the darkest night, God shines a light," he used to say.

She smiled and turned toward the house, when she glimpsed something out of the corner of her eye. Something flew between her and the moon. Her poor eyesight was slow in revealing details, but as the object neared the clearing, she could see—a man with wings, an angel—heading straight toward her.

"He's come for me," she whispered.

The majestic figure descended at the yard's edge, its translucent wings sweeping before its chest to slow its descent. Bare feet touched the grass without a sound, and the figure walked, slowly but steadily, toward her.

When the being came within ten feet, Rose could see more clearly. The winged figure was an emaciated, naked thing, its ribs visible as it turned momentarily toward the moonlight.

For an instant, it hesitated, as if it had changed its mind about approaching her. Then, it moved closer and opened wide its arms to welcome an embrace.

"Sweet Jesus," Rose said and rushed into its waiting arms. "You've come back to me."

The thing with Samuel Vance's visage wrapped its arms around Rose's waist, and from somewhere in its simple mind came the instinctive impulse to run the fingers of its right hand tenderly through her thin grey hair.

Blinded with joy, she did not notice how cold, how hard her late husband's chest had become, or how the hairs of his arms had been replaced with thick, stiff barbs. All that mattered was that her prayers had been answered. Samuel had returned for her.

Without warning, the creature yanked back on Rose's hair. She stumbled backward, and he snapped out with his left hand. His long, razor sharp claws slashed across her throat.

18

Blood gushed out in spurts, but Rose did not scream. She felt no fear, just total acceptance of the method which her beloved had chosen to remove her from this troubled world.

The last thing Rose saw was the lips parting on her late husband's expressionless face. As she passed out, a long, tubular tongue with a narrow barbed tip uncoiled from his toothless mouth. The tip slid into her severed jugular vein, and like a butterfly feeding upon nectar, he drained all the blood from her frail body.

# CHAPTER 4

Steve sat on the couch and unlaced his work boots. The phone rang.

"Hello."

"Hey, Steve. Hear what happened last night?"

"No, Mike. I've been up on the mountain all day. We set off a shot late this evening, and I just got home."

"We had a murder last night—preacher Vance's widow."

"What happened?"

"We're not sure. Her throat was cut. We found her in her back yard. Funny thing is, there was hardly any blood on the scene. The corner's preliminary report says all the blood's been drained from her body."

"How did the killer manage that?"

"I can't figure it—unless somebody used some type of pump to siphon it out."

"Do you think there's a connection between the murder and the missing body?"

"Definitely. But I don't have the foggiest notion what it might be. I went back to the cemetery today. Rose's grandson and great grandson had the gate open; they were digging her grave by hand with shovels and a pick."

"Had the Vance boys seen anything?"

"Not a thing."

"No clues at the cemetery—any at the murder site?"

"Not a one. It's like the killer appeared and disappeared into thin air."

# CHAPTER 5

"How much farther boys?" Mike asked the two teenaged hunters and wiped sweat from his brow.

It had been nearly four months since Rose Vance had been laid to rest beside the empty gravesite of her beloved Samuel. The sheriff had called the State Police in to aid in the murder investigation and the search for the missing body, but nothing had turned up in either case—until now.

Hours ago, the dispatcher had called the sheriff with a report that two young squirrel hunters had discovered the remains of a male body deep in the woods. Mike stopped by the hospital to pick up a body bag before proceeding to his rendezvous with the boys along a gravel road.

"Not getting tired are you, sheriff?" one of the boys asked Mike when he stopped to rest against a tree trunk. They had climbed for twenty minutes up the steep slope of a heavily forested mountain.

"Just catching my breath," Mike said. "I've got fifteen years and fifty pounds on you boys."

"We're almost there," the other boy said. "It's just over the next rise."

The three resumed their climb, and minutes later, one of the boys pointed at an open space between two trees.

"There—against one of those trees," the boy said.

The sheriff rushed ahead. He found, leaning against the base of a beech tree, the withered remains of something which resembled a human being. The grey, naked figure was devoid of lips and eyes; the vultures had obviously already paid their respects.

Mike studied the remains; the face and body structure resembled a skinny old man, but there were definite non-humanoid features. Two antennae on either side of the head, each more than a foot long. The fingers and toes culminated in curved, two-inch long claws. Black barbs, thick as pencil leads, covered the arms and legs like a sparse growth of body hair. The smooth, grey skin segmented at every joint. Most bizarre were the stubby, chewed-off remains of translucent wings that extended for a foot or more behind each shoulder.

The boys stood beside the sheriff. "What kind of thing is this?" one said. "We didn't stay long enough to get a good look at it before," the other boy said.

"I don't have any idea," Mike said. But he knew who this creature used to be. Samuel Vance's body had been found.

"Give me a hand with this thing," Mike said. He stretched out the body bag and unzipped it alongside the creature.

Each boy grabbed an ankle and Mike lifted the stiff, bony arms above its head.

"It feels like rubber," one of the boys said as he lowered the remains into the bag.

"Maybe that's what it is," Mike said. "Somebody is trying to play a trick on us." He hoped that would satisfy their curiosity and head off gossip.

"It wasn't too heavy, was it?" one boy said as Mike zipped the bag shut. "Couldn't weigh more than 50 pounds."

"And it didn't stink like something dead would have; did you notice?" the other said.

"You're right," Mike said. "If it was real, it would've been stinking up the whole mountain."

"What're you going to do with it?"

"Give it to the Jaycees for their haunted house next month," Mike said. He gestured for one of the boys to grab the other end of the bag, and they headed down the mountain.

# CHAPTER 6

After Mike loaded the remains into the trunk of his cruiser, his first thought was to drive to the mountaintop mining operation to share his find with Steve.

When he arrived at the mine, Steve was sitting in his truck watching a road grader clean out a ditch line. Mike pulled alongside the Jeep and rolled his window down.

"You won't believe what I've got in my trunk."

"Jimmy Hoffa's body?"

"Nope. Better than that—Preacher Vance's."

"Where'd you find him?"

"Get in and I'll tell you. You won't believe me until you see it."

Mike drove to an isolated logging road adjoining the mining operation. The two exited the car, and Mike popped open the trunk.

"Here it is." He gestured proudly toward the body bag.

"Do I need to cover my nose?"

"No, I don't think so. It wasn't stinking when we found it in the woods."

Mike hurriedly unzipped the bag and stepped back to

reveal the contents.

"What the hell—?" Steve said, startled by the gaunt, grey form. "It does resemble the picture I saw of Sam. What's this sticking out past the shoulder?"

"Looks like piece of a wing. There's another one on the other side. Scavengers must have gnawed the rest of the wings off . . ."

"Along with his lips and eyeballs," Steve said. "Pretty gross. Have you told anybody about this?"

"No. I wanted to give you first peek."

"Could you keep it at your place, just overnight?" Steve said. "I want to call Alan in on this."

"That could cost me my job, concealing—"

"Concealing what? A dead body that's sprouted wings a year after it was buried?"

"Ok. Call Alan. I can't wait to get this thing off my hands."

# CHAPTER 7

Two weeks later.

Fort Detrick, Frederick, Maryland. Headquarters for the United States Army Medical Research Institute of Infectious Diseases (USAMRIID). A tall man dressed in a black suit, white shirt, and black tie knocked once on an office door, then twisted the knob without awaiting a reply. Inside, he faced a dark haired woman in a white lab coat seated behind a desk along the back of the tiny office.

"What have you concluded?" he said.

The woman stood and offered her hand.

"Dr. Donna McKenzie, entomologist. And you're Special Agent Alan Smith," she said, pointing at his photo ID card.

Agent Smith gripped her hand. "Pleased to meet you. About code name Dragonfly . . ."

"Obviously, you're as fascinated as I am about this find."

"Obviously," Agent Smith said. "What is it? I'm no physician, but that thing they hauled out of the woods looked organic to me."

"It's organic, all right. Once as much alive as you or I."

"It looked like a cross between a human and an insect."

"It's a mix of human and something," she said. "I sent a tissue sample to the genetics lab. They found 30 pairs of chromosomes, all 23 common to Homo sapiens, and seven that have never been identified before."

"Meaning?"

"The remaining DNA is not of earthly origin."

"You're saying it's from an extraterrestrial source? I don't think I can buy that."

"I'm not trying to sell you. I can't speculate how the two DNA types came together."

"Maybe a human screwed an alien, and this hybrid was the result?" Agent Smith posited facetiously.

"More like the alien DNA screwed over the human DNA. You won't believe me unless I show you. Do you feel like playing dress-up?"

"I've never been inside one of those yellow space suits before, but yeah, I'm game."

"Follow me, then. We'll get suited up and enter the Biosafety Level 4 Labs."

"Was this necessary?" he said.

The agent squirming inside the yellow biohazard "space suit" reminded Dr. McKenzie of a child trying to slither out an itchy wool sweater. The image made her smile.

"I'm the one who zipped it inside the body bag and crated it up to be sent here," he said. "If it were carrying some kind of disease, wouldn't I have come down with it by now?"

"I don't know enough about this thing to answer that. Since I've sliced it open, there is a definite risk of exposure to bodily fluids."

She led him to a covered steel table, then yanked off the

black plastic cover, exposing the creature's autopsied remains.

"Nice incision," Agent Smith said, staring at the wound that ran from the neck to the groin region.

"I used a laser scalpel. Couldn't slice through the skin with my sharpest blades . . . put a section of its hide under the microscope. Never seen anything like it. It resembles a fabric weave more than skin. Organic Kevlar, you might say."

"See these?" She indicated the two narrow, sixteen-inch long antennae at the top of the being's head. "If you look closely, you'll see tiny hairs on either side of the antennae. Each hair is covered with microscopic setae that pass messages on to the central nervous system. In the insect world, you'll find these sensory organs on moths and several other winged species."

"What type of sensing could it do with these?"

"For some insects, it provides touch, taste, hearing and an acute sense of smell. Cecropia moths, for instance, can detect minute traces from a plume of another moth's sexual pheromones from three miles or more away. I suspect this fellow had similar capabilities, but we can't be certain unless we find a living one to study."

"We both should be so lucky."

Dr. McKenzie picked up a penlight flashlight from a counter top and shined the beam onto what should have been the ear cavity.

"Notice there is no longer an ear canal. The outer parts of the ear are all that remain. Just so much window dressing. Inside the head, nothing resembling an ear canal.

"I won't roll the body over to show you my incision through the skull. Here are some photos of what I found." She handed him a stack of Polaroids from the counter.

"The brain is not much larger than a walnut. The

trilobe brain is the culmination of a spinal cord that runs from the head to the groin region."

"What about the remaining space inside the skull?" Smith said.

"There wasn't that much extra space. The brain floated in hemolymph, or in layman's terms, insect blood. The rest of the space inside the head, well, that can most easily be shown here in the sternum."

She pulled aside the skin flaps to either side of the long incision down the center of the chest, revealing the breast bone.

"Looks like bone, doesn't it? There isn't a single bit of bone in this guy's entire body. This stuff looks like bone, and occurs in every place that bone would be in the human body, but it's all hollow."

She picked up a thin cross section of white material from alongside the being's body on the steel table.

"This is a section I cut from the femur of the left leg. It resembles dried cellulose from dead weeds, if you've ever taken a look at such things . . ."

"I have," Smith said. "When you grow up deep in the country, you have time to notice such stuff."

"We have something in common. I grew up on a farm in—"

"What is this "bone" material made of?" Smith said.

"Based on initial analysis, I'd say that it's the equivalent of the chitin that makes up an insect's exoskeleton—chitin being a tough polysaccharide that resembles the cellulose and starch found in plants. Lab tests revealed several proteins commonly found in the insect chitin, among them sclerotin, a protein that causes the insect's outer skin to harden.

"The beastie's outer skin is also a form of chitin, albeit less concentrated than the stuff that has replaced the human skeleton. The outer hide has various lipids and waxes throughout that serve to waterproof the skin, but other chemicals have provided an elasticity that isn't present in the stiff, individual plates that make up an insect's exoskeleton. In a typical insect, flexible membranes between the individual plates make movement possible, but this thing's outer cuticle is quite pliable."

"What do we have beneath the rib cage?"

Dr. McKenzie lifted the severed sternum and several ribs from the chest cavity, revealing—not much of anything.

"Inside, we have a typical insect's innards," she said. "The open circulatory system consists of the dorsal vessel, which is this long, hollow tube that runs from the groin to the base of the brain, and this drying goo, which was the hemolymph that filled the cavity. All his internal organs floated in this volume of blood.

"The large muscle of the dorsal vessel near the head is the aorta. The muscle on the section of the dorsal vessel down here in the stomach is the heart. These muscles forced blood from the heart to the head. Then, the blood flowed again into the chest cavity and back into the heart through these tiny openings, the ostia. There are no arteries or veins, to speak of. The organs and tissue were directly bathed in blood."

"How did it breathe?" Smith said. "I don't see any lungs."

"Respiration is the same as in insects. These small holes on both sides of the body are like the spiracles of an insect. Oxygen enters through the spiracle, then passes into small tubes, called trachea. The trachea can expand or contract to form air sacs. The creature's stomach muscles pumped involuntarily to push air through the trachea system.

"The digestive, excretive, and reproductive systems are

also common to those found in insects."

"Dr. McKenzie, are you saying this thing was capable of reproducing with that dilapidated looking piece of equipment?"

"Aren't jealous, are we?"

"Of that? No way—trust me."

"I'll take your word on it." Her glance never left the creature's remains. "There's more there than meets the eye. Yes, I believe this human-shaped phallus also served as the creature's sex organ. But with insects, appearances can often be deceiving. One of the most fascinating things about insects is that their body parts are often not found where we humans expect them to be. For instance, the gills for the dragonfly larvae are found within the rectum . . .

"Sorry, I'm rambling. Back to the penis. Unlike in humans, it was not the source of elimination for liquid waste for this fellow—his hindgut probably absorbed water for recycling within the system. This organ resembles a segmented, telescoping rod, capable of extending to lengths two and one-half to three times that of its human counter-part. Sperm was produced in testes, actually located deeper within the body rather than in this human looking—"

"I think I've seen more than enough," Smith said. "I can't wait to get out of this oversized baggie."

After grumbling through the decontamination procedure (which included walking in the suit beneath a shower of disinfectant), Agent Smith joined Dr. McKenzie in her office.

"You've examined the photos and death certificate I sent of the Reverend Vance?" Smith said. Dr. McKenzie nodded.

"Did this insect-gutted thing used to be Mr. Vance?" he said.

"Yes. Improbable as it seems, I believe this thing originated within Mr. Vance. I had a computer analysis performed of Mr. Vance's photo and an image of the creature. With the exception of the antennae on the top of the head and a slight sharpening of the jaw line, the two images overlaid perfectly."

"Was the good reverend the victim of a parasite?"

"Not in any normal sense of the word. A parasite, or more correctly a parasitoid, is usually a smaller organism that is attached to the interior or the exterior of the host organism. As the parasitoid grows, it usually eats away at the host's body, resulting in the host's death. The parasitoid, after eating its fill, emerges from the host's carcass. If Mr. Vance's death certificate is accurate, he died of natural causes, and not from the damaged caused by a parasitoid."

"Then when did this creature infect the man's remains?"

"I assume he was buried inside a modern, sealed coffin?" McKenzie said.

"And the coffin was sealed inside a concrete vault," Smith said.

"Then this creature apparently took up residence within Mr. Vance sometime before his death."

"But when, and by what method?"

"You're the investigator. You tell me. However, I do have a far-out theory."

"Let's hear it."

"What if this creature was like an egg that had been planted inside Mr. Vance's body, and it waited, perhaps for months or years, for the right conditions to incubate?"

"What could these conditions be? Something related to what happens to a human body at death?" Smith said.

"Exactly. If I remember correctly, one thing that happens after death is a rise in levels of lactic acid, and a few hours later, a rapid increase in bacteria levels in the intestines—that is, if the body isn't embalmed in a timely manner."

"So the increased, sustained levels of lactic acid could've been the signal for the alien egg to start incubation," Smith said.

"Could be. From that point, the alien DNA somehow, over the space of one year, transformed the human bone and tissue to what we've just seen."

"But why is the exterior a spitting image of a human being?"

"Perhaps the epidermis of human skin serves as a signal that establishes the transformation boundaries. Image the benefits for the alien organism. It finds itself developing inside an unknown organism in an alien environment. What better way to fit into that strange environment than to assume the form of an organism native to that environment?"

"Sounds like a lot of sci-fi gobbledygook to me," Smith said.

"That's the best I can do on speculation. Give me a live specimen, a team of scientists, and a few months and maybe I can offer you something better."

"Talk to your bosses in the Pentagon. I've turned over all we have."

"I'd like to visit the grave site this thing emerged from," Dr. McKenzie said.

"I think I can arrange that." Agent Smith buttoned his suit coat and reached for the door knob. "I'll be in touch."

Agent Smith arranged for his brother, Steve, to pick Dr. McKenzie up on Saturday at the nearest airport.

"How will I recognize her?" Steve had asked.

"Tall, slender woman. Five feet eight. She has short

cropped black hair. Green eyes. Approximately 30 years of age," Alan said.

"She made an impression," Steve said.

"It goes with the job."

"Yeah, right. Sounds easy on the eyes."

"I thought so."

# CHAPTER 8

One of the first passengers off the small turbo prop plane was a tall, dark haired woman dressed in matching brown khaki jeans and shirt. She bounded down the steps like a grade school child getting off a school bus on the last day of school, swinging a small bag in her right hand.

"Donna McKenzie?" Steve said as she walked through the gate.

"Yes, you must be Steve."

"Pleased to meet you. How was your flight?"

"Very turbulent. Is it always like that coming into these mountains?"

"I wouldn't know. I—don't fly."

"Sometimes I wish I didn't, but it's a must in my line of work."

"Let's retrieve your bags."

He loaded two small pieces of luggage into the back seat of his SUV, and they headed off on the seventy mile trip to Reverend Vance's grave.

"Agent Smith tells me you're a mining engineer. Do you have to spend a lot of time underground?"

"Thankfully, no. None at all. I'm the superintendent for Black Diamond's surface mining operations. I've been underground on a couple of occasions—definitely not to my liking." She noticed something—a sense of dread, perhaps—in the way that he said it.

A moment of uncomfortable silence ensued, then Steve resumed the conversation. "I understand you're an entomologist. Where did you train for that?"

"University of Illinois, Department of Entomology. I studied under the noted entomologist Gilbert Waldbauer. I don't suppose you've heard of him?"

"No, afraid not."

"It's not a very glamorous occupation, but I thrive on the variety and the travel. I switched majors half way through med school."

"So you have a background in humans and bugs?" Steve said.

"Yes. That's probably why the government called me in on this project."

"So, what was that thing?"

"I assume your brother told you that I wouldn't be able to discuss specifics?"

"Yeah. Can't blame me for trying. I know one thing—it was for real."

"Why do you say that?"

"This isn't Hollywood. Nobody in these parts could create such a thing. I believe it killed Preacher Vance's widow."

"Agent Smith's report indicated that possibility. Do the locals know about your find?"

"Nobody but a couple of kids who found the carcass, and, of course, my old buddy, Sheriff Mike Stollard."

"Anyone else in on it?"

"No. Alan told me and Mike to keep it under our hats."

"Good. We don't need anyone mudding the waters."

"What will you be looking for?"

"I won't know until I find it," Dr. McKenzie said.

After leaving the mountaintop airport, they drove onto a four-lane highway. To either side of the road were gently rolling hills.

"This reminds me of home," she said.

"Where's that?"

"Wisconsin. I grew up on a farm."

"Big family?"

"Only child. Dad wanted a boy, but I didn't disappoint him much. I was a real tomboy. Always out playing with the boys, turning over rocks and playing with bugs."

"Is that why you chose your field?"

"Partially. There were practical reasons, too. Insects can be a farmer's worst enemy. I spent a couple of years at the Research Triangle Park in North Carolina working on improving pesticides."

"That may come in handy with our new pest."

"How about you?" Donna said. "You from around here?"

"Yeah. All my life. Born and bred. You see those mountains?" Steve pointed to a mountain range looming in the distance. "That's where I come from."

"Majestic," she said.

"From a distance. But they're not so pretty when you're stuck down in the middle of them. They have a way of suffocating you. They've kept us in—and most people out—for hundreds of years."

"Why have you stayed?"

"I wish I knew. Familiarity, maybe. Fear of the unknown? I don't know. I spend a lot of time mining the tops off of mountains. Maybe I'm at war with them, and I have to be where the fighting is."

"Deep," she said.

"Too deep. We're about to run out of straight road."

Steve flicked his turn signal and turned onto an exit ramp. "Hope your lunch has had time to settle. These mountain roads have been known to empty the stomachs of flatlanders."

"I'll be fine if I keep my eyes on the road and pretend I'm doing the driving."

After a half hour on a winding, narrow two lane pavement, Steve turned off onto a rough gravel road. Fifteen minutes later, they arrived at the mountaintop cemetery.

Steve put the vehicle in park and unlocked the gate to the cemetery with a key attached to a retractable loop on his belt. He pushed the heavy pipe gate to the side of the road and returned to the vehicle.

"It's just over the top of this hill," he said.

Momentarily, they arrived at the tree lined cemetery.

"Mr. and Mrs. Vance are buried on the other side of that new marble headstone," Steve said, pointing to a spot about twenty feet away. "I'll bring a shovel."

She waited for him by the gravesite.

"His children did a good job of repairing the damage," Steve said. "There was a circular hole about 12 inches in diameter that went all the way down through the vault and into the casket. It was just about the center of the grave mound.

"I'm kind of curious how they plugged the hole," he said. He started scooping shovelfuls of earth. A few inches down, the shovel struck something solid. He dusted off the soil with his hands.

"They've covered the hole with a rock," he said, prying

the stone away with the shovel blade tip.

He stepped back from the grave and leaned upon the shovel handle. "Be my guest."

Dr. McKenzie kneeled over the grave and shined a flashlight into the smooth, circular hole. "Amazing, isn't it?" she said. "Looks like it was done by a machine."

"That's what the preacher's family—"

"I think I see something," she said. "Do you have something that can reach down to the bottom?"

"I have a set of post-hole diggers in the Jeep.

"I didn't see anything when I looked in before," he said as he carried the post-hole digger from the vehicle. "It looked like the coffin lining to me."

"No, the texture wasn't right. Can you bring a sample up with those?"

"Let's see how far I can reach."

Steve eased the metal bucket and its wooden handles into the hole and slid both his arms about 18 inches into the hole.

"I've hit the bottom," he said. He pulled the two wooden handles as far apart as the hole's narrow confines would allow. "I hope that's enough to get a bite off the bottom."

He pulled the digger back out and rested its bucket on a stone.

"I think we've got something," she said.

Steve shoved the handles toward each other and tapped the bucket on the ground, spilling a handful of thick, purple matter.

"God, that stinks," Steve said. "What the hell is it?"

Dr. McKenzie had already pulled on a pair of rubber gloves and dropped a mask over her nose and mouth.

"Some species of insects defecate when their bodies emerge from the nymph to the adult stage," she said, pushing a large sample with a stick into a specimen jar.

"A pile of bug crap?"

"Yes, that and hopefully some clues to the physiology of the thing that crawled out of that hole."

"Are you ready for me to seal it up?"

"I've got a good sample."

Steve carefully replaced the cover stone and soil.

"Ready to get off the mountain?" he said.

"No, I want to look around in the woods for awhile."

"What are you looking for? Don't tell me—you'll know when you find it."

"You're reading me like a book."

"I'll wait by the vehicle. Don't wander too far; we killed a few rattle snakes when we mined around this area."

"I'm not afraid of snakes. Remind me to tell you about my adventures in the Amazon rainforest."

"I'll do that." Steve watched her enter the clearing at the cemetery's edge. Quite a spunky lady, he thought.

# CHAPTER 9

Steve checked in with his office on his cell phone, then sat in the vehicle listening to the call of nearby birds and the distance clatter of bulldozers removing overburden from the coal seam on the next ridgetop.

Just as he closed his eyes to enjoy the relative solitude, Donna said, "Holy shit! Steve, get over here!"

Steve joined Donna on the knob's north side at the base of a tall locust tree. "What have you found?"

"Look on the back of this tree."

About eight feet up the tree, Steve saw two light brown objects that looked like the bottoms of a man's feet.

"Good God!" Steve gasped. "Have they hanged someone in the tree?"

"No. Step back a bit and look through between these limbs."

Though it looked like a man, it was not Samuel Vance's corpse. Nor was it his skin, though that was certainly what it could have been, had it been possible to strip it off his flesh and have it still retain its shape.

The hollow shell clinging to the tree looked exactly like

the deceased Baptist preacher. The shape of Samuel Vance faced the tree, with both hands, one higher than the other, in front of the head. It was as if the shell had crawled like a cat up the bark.

The head, nearly fifteen feet above the ground, faced right; the lips were sealed and the eyes were open, staring expressionlessly toward the neighboring trees. Other than the fingernails and toenails, nothing anchored the figure to the tree.

A long slit down the back of the thin, light brown shell extended from just below the back of the neck to the small of the back.

"What kind of prank is this?" Steve said.

"I have an idea. You know what it reminds me of? The seventeen year cicadas when they come out of the ground."

"I remember," Steve said. "They come out and climb up a tree. Their outer shell dries and splits open in the back. They dry their wings out and fly away into the trees to start mating. Of course, you probably know a lot more about them than I do. They swarmed around here about seven or eight years ago."

"They're great, aren't they?" Dr. McKenzie beamed. "They were in Wisconsin when I was about ten. I think they were my earliest inspiration to get into this line of work."

"I love those critters. They fascinate the heck out of me. But what do the cicadas have to do with this thing?"

"There may be some similar transformational process at work."

"Do you want to cut a piece out of it?" Steve pulled a pocket knife out of his left front pants pocket. "I'll boost you up on my shoulders, and you can cut a piece of this thing off to analyze."

Steve kneeled before the tree, and Donna stepped onto

his shoulders. The extra height enabled her to reach as far as the calf of one leg of the shell.

"I've got hold of it," she said.

"Can you yank the whole thing down from there?"

Donna tugged on one of the brown shell's ankles.

"No go. This thing's like it's been nailed to the bark."

She poked the knife into the shell's calf, to no avail; the knife tip slid off to the side. "This stuff's a lot tougher than it looks," she said. "I can't cut through it. Ease me down."

Steve squatted, and Dr. McKenzie jumped to the ground.

"I want the whole molt," she said.

"I have a chain saw in the back of my vehicle," Steve said.

He fired up the saw and cut about half way through the trunk. The tree crackled as it split on the side opposite the notch cut, then slowly fell to the ground. A strand of wood held the two tree parts together. He cut the tree off just above the shell's hands, and while Donna held that end in her lap, he finished severing the lower end from the tree stump.

"Think we can carry this out of here?" he said.

"I can carry my end if you can."

"Fair enough. Let's get this in the truck."

When they made it back to the vehicle, they placed their prize on the open tailgate. Steve pushed down on one side of the split in the back of the shell and found it flexible. "Reminds me of a piece of leather," he said.

"Yes," Donna said. "But a lot tougher to cut."

She opened a piece of her luggage and removed two long, black plastic bags and a bundle of twine.

"Looks like you expected to find this," Steve said.

"Not exactly. If I'd known, I'd have brought a bigger bag."

They slid a bag over each end of the log and the human-shaped skin, and secured the overlapping bags with a piece of twine in the center.

"Let's go for a bite to eat," she said.

"You can still eat—after seeing this?"

"Ravenously."

"So, Dr. McKenzie," Steve said as he sliced a knife into his steak, "what does our find tell you about our late friend?"

"Please, call me Donna. The molt tells me several things. The shed skin's shape is identical to the remains of the specimen lying on the table in my lab, which means that the pre-adult stage was identical to the adult which emerged after the molt, and both are nearly identical to the human being, Mr. Vance, that the thing started from."

"Which tells you what?"

"I'm not sure. I've been trying to put a theory together. Let's start with the basics. If we consider the development stages of an insect—which the autopsy I performed leads me to believe we must—my theory goes something like this. The typical insect experiences complete metamorphosis, which means four stages: egg, larva, pupa, and adult. The larva is the growing or food procuring stage. The pupa is the transformation stage in which the larva transforms into an adult which is usually very different in size and appearance.

"Other insects, like dragonflies, roaches, and our favorites, the cicada, go through an incomplete metamorphosis of only three distinct stages: egg, nymph, and adult. There is no transformation, or pupa stage leading from nymph to adult. The nymph and adult basically, except for slight size differences and development of wings, look the same."

45

"So we may be talking intergalactic cicada here?" Steve said.

"The molt and the fact that it bored out of the ground are common to the earthly cicada, but there are similarities to other insect species—parasites, in particular. Parasites, such as some species of wasps, lay their eggs either on or directly into the body of the dead or paralyzed host insect. The developing larvas usually consume the body of their host, but that isn't what's happened here with our emergent. Whatever entered Mr. Vance's body totally transformed his insides, while leaving his outer shape intact."

"Any ideas on how the egg got into his body?"

"Your brother and I pondered this last week. He was buried in a metal casket sealed inside a concrete vault, so it's highly unlikely it happened after burial. My guess is the egg entered and anchored itself to his body while he was living, but how and when are beyond me at this point. If the egg were present prior to death, it is possible that physical changes that occur in the body at death, such as a sustained level of lactic acid, may have been the trigger that started the egg's development."

"You think these things have targeted humans as their hosts?"

"Not necessarily. It may be that humans are simply the most fertile soil, so to speak, to plant the eggs in."

"How so?"

"If this egg, in fact, does not begin to develop until its host dies, and the period of development is approximately 12 months, the body of other animals, say a dog or a bear, would rot long before the egg could complete its developmental stages. Since human bodies are usually embalmed and buried in dry environments, that would make Homo sapiens uniquely qualified to serve as

46

incubators and nutrient sources for the emergents. When digger wasps, for example, attach their egg to a host, they prepare a dry burrow to provide an environment that will preserve their egg and its host—"

"That's twice you've used that word."

"What?"

"Emergents. You like it, don't you?" Steve said.

"Yes. Kinda catchy. I think it's appropriate for a creature that defies and crosses all existing classification criteria."

"You were hired by the FBI to study this emergent?"

"I'm . . . not supposed to say. I've said enough already to get you and me both in serious trouble."

"Don't worry about it," Steve said. "Alan swore me to secrecy; he wouldn't have had me bring you down here unless he felt he could trust me. What do you think the government wants out of this? I mean, if it's strictly scientific, wouldn't the National Science Foundation or some such have sent you?"

"If this thing is of extraterrestrial origin, as I think it is, it's a matter of national security. Beyond that, well, I'm always a cynic when it comes to the military. I think the Pentagon is hoping for some sort of military application for this thing."

"What kind of weapon could you make of a thing that reanimates dead bodies?"

"A frightening one. Let's assume that the development period from egg to adult could be greatly shortened in some way. Could you imagine the havoc that would be wreaked behind enemy lines during a long military conflict if thousands of those things should pop out of battlefield graves and start drinking the blood of living troops?"

"That thing did drink every drop out of Mrs. Vance.

Ironic that his widow was its only victim—as far as we know. Why didn't it kill more? And what killed it?"

"Maybe one was all it needed."

"For what—food?"

"Maybe. Or perhaps to charge its sperms."

"You mean that thing was capable of reproducing?"

"Oh, yes. You might say it was very well equipped. All it needed was a female emergent to start replicating itself. Perhaps the adult stage is limited to a very brief life span—"

"Like the periodical cicadas?" Steve said. "They live underground, munching on roots for 17 years, and only live for a few weeks after they mate."

"Which is a sight longer than some species of the poor mayfly, which emerges and mates, or attempts to mate, and then dies, either way, within twenty-four hours after it begins its adult life. Copulation or no copulation, our guy was on a short clock."

"Do you think he flew? It scares the hell out of me to imagine thousands of those things dropping down from the sky."

"Based upon the mass of muscle I found attached to its wing pads, I'd have to say yes. It may have been possible for him to generate his own lift, just as bumble bees do. Due to his redesigned innards and skeletal structure, I estimate he weighed just over a third of what his human host weighed."

"And you know how hard it is to kill a tiny wasp."

"Hundreds of times easier than to kill this fellow. His skin would be nearly bullet proof, and even if you penetrated his body, his blood would have instantly sealed any small bullet holes. I hate to sound so pessimistic, but some insects have been known to live for days after their heads has been severed from their—"

Conversation ceased as the waitress delivered two slices of apple pie with coffee to their table.

"You're doing wonders for my digestion, Donna."

"Sorry. Oh, I just realized—I didn't make reservations for tonight. Where do you recommend I stay?"

"There are only a couple of places in town, and I hear they've got some of the biggest roaches you've ever seen—in your line of work, that may be an added attraction."

"Not in my sleeping quarters. And I doubt they could compare to the hissing cockroaches of Madagascar. Any other possibilities?"

"Well, if you're interested, I have an extra bedroom at my house—I promise I won't try anything."

"Then, why should I want to come over?" She looked serious for a moment, then smiled and gave his hand a quick squeeze. "Just kidding. I know I can trust you."

"How do you know that?"

"I just have a good feeling about you."

"Do you always go with your feelings?"

"They haven't steered me wrong yet."

"So, you're coming over?"

"Can you get me to the airport for a 9 a.m. flight?"

"I guarantee it."

"Then you've got a house guest, Mr. Smith."

Donna followed Steve up the steps to his second story apartment. He removed his mail from a wall mounted box, unlocked the door, flipped on the lights, and gestured for Donna to enter.

"Welcome. I hope the place isn't too messy for you."

Donna took the room in at a glance. A few fishing magazines were scattered on one end of the couch. No photographs of girlfriends—or anyone else—on display. The end tables could have used a good dusting, but there were no dirty garments on the floor, no unappealing odors. Overall, it was cleaner than most bachelor pads she had visited.

Steve pointed out the doors to the bathroom and spare bedroom. "My bedroom is over here, but we won't open that door. Someday, you may want to conduct a field trip in there, maybe classify the creatures living on the pizza scraps under my bed."

"I doubt it's anywhere as bad as you say."

"For now, it'll be a mystery."

"For now," she said.

# CHAPTER 10

James Evans and his wife Mona had been married, relatively happily, for nearly twenty years—until James lost his job at the coal preparation plant. Despondent, he started drinking heavily, and Mona, who worked at a local grocery, began nagging him to find another job. His resentment grew daily, until he found a drinking partner in Bertha, a twenty-five-year-old divorcee who lived in a rental house next door.

While his wife was away at work, he was able to enjoy Bertha and his beer in peace. Most of the time, they had a midday rendezvous at her place, but now, a few days before Thanksgiving, they had ended up in James and Mona's bed.

After his climax, James rolled off Bertha and onto his back. He wiped sweat from his forehead with the back of his hand.

Bertha lay on her side facing him and circled her fingers through the thick hair of his protruding beer belly.

"James, I don't feel right about this."

"About six months too late to be worrying about it,

ain't it?"

"No. I mean right about doing this here, in your bed. We're taking unnecessary chances. What if your wife comes home and finds us?"

"How many times you seen her come home for lunch?"

"None. But there's a first time for everything. We could've waited until we got to my place."

"I couldn't have made it across the street, bad as I was wanting you." He reached for a beer can on the night stand and found it empty.

"How's about bringing us a couple of cold ones, honey."

She picked up a damp towel from the bed post, wrapped it around herself, and turned to leave the room, but was startled to find herself face-to-face with Mrs. Evans, standing in the bedroom doorway with a long butcher knife raised above her shoulder.

"You dirty bitch. In my own bedroom," Mona said. She lunged at Bertha with the knife, but the younger woman ducked, dropped her towel, and fled naked out of the house.

Mona's forward momentum carried her onto the bed, the knife's blade plunging deep into the mattress at her husband's feet. James jumped out of bed and pulled a revolver from the top draw of the night stand.

"Put the damned knife down, Mona," he said, pointing the pistol at her chest.

Mona yanked the blade out of the mattress and lunged toward him. A shot rang out, and Mona fell backward off the bed, with a bullet hole in the center of her chest.

James stood over her lifeless body and shook his head. "Look what you made me do, Mona." He opened his mouth, placed the barrel of the gun inside, and pulled the trigger.

James and Mona were buried side by side in the Evans family cemetery, less than half a mile from the house where they had lived.

One year later, on a frosty November night, the frozen earth in front of James Evans' tombstone heaved. Two pale grey hands erupted from the burial mound, and the grave gave birth to the seed which had been planted twelve months before. The naked form which had once been James Evans crawled slowly across adjoining graves on its way to the forest bordering the cemetery.

Upon attaining the base of an old oak tree, the creature raised its head, then plunged its long, claw like fingernails into the tree trunk and pulled itself slowly, crab like, up the tree. Its toe claws joined in the effort, and within a few moments, the thing had secured itself half way up the tall tree.

A few hours later, back muscles rippled, then convulsed. A narrow crack appeared between the shoulder blades, then widened as grey flesh pushed its way, ever so slowly, out of the dry, brown shell.

Within an hour, the emergence was complete. The new being hung upside down from the claws on its feet, its face resting against the tree's bark. Increased blood flow to the upper back region, along with air pumped into veins of the tracheal system, unfurled two pairs of delicate, overlapping, damp wings in the cold night air. The wings shined with a metallic iridescence in the moonlight.

Just before dawn, a second being emerged, this time from the grave of Mona Evans. It, too, made its way to the forest, climbed a tree, molted its brown skin, and unfurled and dried its wings.

By noon, the two had met for the first time in their new life, ready to begin carrying out their biological imperative.

Just before his death, James had, unbeknownst to his wife, revised his will, leaving their home and all its contents, along with fifteen thousand in a savings account, to his girlfriend, Bertha. Within a month after James and Mona's funeral, Bertha moved into their house. In the last year, she had entertained several male drinking companions. Chester Fife, a tall, lanky eighteen-year-old, was tonight's bed partner.

After having sex with Chester, Bertha rolled across the bed toward the night stand and reached for a pack of cigarettes.

"Damn. Empty," she said. "Chester, would you be a dear and go out to the car and bring us in a carton of smokes?"

Chester pulled on his briefs, yanked up his jeans, and started out the door.

Bertha tossed his t-shirt and hit him in the back with it.

"Better put that on," she said. "You'll catch your death going out there barechested."

He complied, obediently pulling the shirt over his head before elbowing open the storm door handle and walking barefooted out the door.

He hurried down the long, frost covered lawn to the car, parked on a small concrete pad adjoining a gravel access road. By the time he reached in to grab the carton of cigarettes from the dash, he was shivering from the cold. Racing back up the hill, he heard a strange sound coming from somewhere in the forest behind the house. The fog rolled in, but the full moon was still visible just above the tree line.

Thope—thope—thope came the increasingly louder sound. He stopped to listen more closely. Suddenly, something emerged from the fog and came between him and the moon—a flying man with large wings that beat furiously to stay aloft.

"Jesus H. Christ! I didn't drink that much."

The thing in the sky spotted Chester and swooped toward him, blocking his path back to the house. In an instant, it was nearly upon him. The young man dashed back down the hill, across the gravel road, and into the underbrush that lined the road. The heavy fog had already settled into the forest, concealing the tree limbs that slapped him across the face and chest.

Soon after attaining the forest, the beating of wings ceased, but Chester continued headlong into the thick fog. He crashed like a frightened deer chased by dogs through the woods. Limbs and barbs from unseen trees had ripped and torn the t-shirt from his body. His feet bled from numerous puncture wounds, but he ignored his injuries and continued charging through the forest. The ground rolled away before him, and he tumbled head first down into a deep ravine.

He rolled for a time before slamming head first into the base of a large tree. He shook his head, stunned for a moment, and lay flat upon his back, gazing at the white sea of fog that engulfed him. Perhaps, he reasoned, if he lay perfectly still, the flying devil wouldn't be able to hear him, and he would be safe, at least until he froze to death in the icy night air.

The thing with the visage of the late James Evans was as blinded by the fog as his human prey, but that did not hinder it in the least. The long antennae on the creature's head swiveled slowly from side to side in the cold mist, gathering in the antenna's setae a microscopic plume of human pheromones that had wafted like invisible smoke from Chester's body as he had staggered through the forest.

If the pheromone trail were not enough, the thousands of tiny hairs across the creature's body provided confirmation, detecting narrow ribbons of warmer air where the fleeing human's body heat had warmed the surrounding cold air.

With its twin pairs of wings folded tightly across its back, the thing swiftly, but nearly silently, made its way across the damp leaves that lined the forest floor. When it came down the steep ravine, it could see him once again; the infrared waves given off by the human's blood revealed Chester's outline against the tree.

The exhausted boy did not hear a thing until the beast stepped on a twig at his feet. By then, flight was futile. The thing pounced upon his chest, pinning him to the ground. With a single slash from its claws, it severed Chester's jugular.

As his life sprayed out of the gash in his throat, his stalker prepared to feast. The thing's lips parted, allowing a long, coiled taper of a tongue to unfurl. Like a butterfly feasting on nectar, the creature slowly drained the protein rich blood from Chester Fife's body. By dawn, its sperm would be charged with nourishment, and mating could proceed.

Seconds after Chester had fled into the forest, a second winged being flew over Bertha's house and landed on the lawn outside her bedroom window. It had been drawn, inexplicably, to this place where it had lived, dormant, as a tiny egg in the body of its human host, Mona Evans.

Attracted to the light coming from the ground level window, it approached the house and peered inside. Its inhuman eyes saw Bertha propped upright on two pillows, covered by a sheet. The mortal Mona would have been enraged anew to find this woman once again in her bed, resting on pillow cases she had sewn by hand, but the mortal Mona had died in this room, just over a year ago. All that remained of Mona was this hungry being that had assumed her visage.

The creature plunged head first through the window. Bertha looked up as the thing with her late rival's face landed in a spray of broken glass on the bed at her feet. She screamed, then long, razor sharp claws pierced her through the throat and pinned her against the bed's headboard. Her body twitched once, then went limp. The female emergent unrolled her proboscis and feasted.

Before dawn, the creatures reunited in sight of the graves from which they had emerged the night before. Their bodies were energized by the blood they had consumed, and it was time to fulfill their genetic directive.

The female emergent climbed near the top of an old pine tree. The male, standing on the ground, waved his antennae, picking up pheromones which told him that she was ready for him. He followed her up the tree and mounted her from behind. In a grotesque, emotionless mockery of human copulation, he thrust repeatedly into his unearthly mate. With a violent shudder, he discharged into her womb.

They remained linked for a time, then he separated from her and crawled down, feet first, from the tree.

His energy was nearly spent. At the moment of orgasm, his body manufactured and released a death hormone. His sole purpose for life fulfilled, he would die quietly in the forest a few hours later.

# CHAPTER 11

Willie Showalter shoveled in loose earth on top of the ammonium nitrate explosive to fill the last drill hole. He connected the hole's shot wires in series with the other holes, then retreated about a hundred yards to the shelter of a large dump truck. He carried a small detonator box under the dump truck bed and pulled a walkie-talkie from his shirt pocket.

"I'm ready to connect the wires to the detonator and set her off, Steve," Willie said.

Steve stood outside his vehicle on the ridge opposite the blast area and pushed down the transmit button on his radio.

"Roger, Willie. You boys go ahead and sound the siren," Steve said.

Other personnel, located in an office trailer further away from the blast zone, responded to the command to sound the warning. There came three long blasts from the siren, then Willie pushed down the plunger.

The explosion shook the earth at Showalter's feet and resounded off the surrounding mountains. Steve smiled with great satisfaction as an orange dust cloud rose above the blast zone, then gradually dissipated in the breeze. The blast had loosened another 20 feet depth of overburden overlying the thick coal seam. Little by little, day by day, the mountain was yielding to the new level contours of his mining plans. After the all clear signal, the end loader and dump trucks would come in to scoop and haul away the shattered stone. Steve jumped in his Jeep and headed toward the mine site.

Willie disconnected the shot wires from his detonator and peered out from under the bed of the huge dump truck. He waited a moment for the smoke to clear, then cautiously approached the blast zone. The overburden was shattered consistently; all the shots had fired successfully.

Willie pulled out his walkie-talkie. "Go ahead and sound the—good lord!"

Glancing up at the forest along the top of the eighty foot highwall above the blast zone, he saw the silhouette against the sun of—could it be—a winged person?

"Willie, what's wrong?" Steve said over the radio.

Before Showalter could reply, the thing which had been Mona Evans swooped upon him and slammed him to the ground. The portable radio flew from his hand. He struggled to break free of the winged creature that sat with its knees upon his chest and its claws slicing into his shoulders. For a moment, it appeared he would be able to push the devil away, but a long stinger flashed from the base of the being's spine and imbedded itself in the man's groin.

The ovipositor injected a paralyzing venom into Willie's groin, then deposited a single, tiny egg into his bloodstream.

The venom instantly took effect. Willie's body went limp beneath his attacker. His breathing and heart rate slowed to dangerously low levels, but he remained conscious, his eyes locked open to stare into the creature's blood red eyes.

He tried to scream, but could not make a sound, could only look on in horror as the naked beast clamped tighter onto his shoulders and flapped its wings furiously. Willie felt himself begin to rise above the ground.

When the creature had lifted its prey about five feet above the earth, a car horn sounded, and Steve's vehicle came speeding toward them. The emergent, startled by the sound, eased its grasp on Willie's shoulders just enough to allow his body to fall free.

Steve stomped on his brakes, narrowly avoiding running over his immobilized co-worker. The thing with the face of Mona Evans buzzed angrily at losing the human incubator for its egg, but surprisingly ignored the men and flew high into the sky, disappearing quickly behind the trees above the highwall.

Steve jumped out of the vehicle, opened a door to the back seat, then dragged the wounded man inside.

"What's happened?" someone said over the radio.

"Willie been stung by a bunch of hornets," Steve said, thinking fast. "I'm going to take him in to the hospital."

Steve sped down the mountain, and within 20 minutes, he arrived at the emergency room of Richville Community Hospital.

"I've got an injured man out here," he told the attendant.

Orderlies and an emergency room physician wheeled Showalter into the hospital.

"Is he still alive?" Steve said.

"He's got a very weak pulse, shallow breathing," the doctor said. "What happened to him?"

"I think something stung him in the underbrush."

"He must be allergic big time," an orderly said.

The orderly pushed Willie around the corner. Steve went outside and dialed his brother at the FBI.

"Alan, you'll never guess what happened just now on the job site."

"You found another grave with a hole drilled in it?"

"Bigger than that. One of my men got attacked by one of those things just after he set off a shot."

"You saw it happen?"

"I didn't see the attack; it was flying away with him when I arrived. It dropped him as I drove up; I must have startled it."

"What kind of shape's he in?"

"Still alive, just barely. Other than some cuts on his shoulders, there weren't any other marks on him. I don't know what it's done to him."

"I'll send one of our doctors to the hospital before dawn to take over his case and collect any blood samples they may have taken."

"You guys can do that?" Steve said.

"Easily. Do me a favor? Can you stay outside his door until one of my agents gets there? If they allow visitors, I want the name of everyone who goes into the room."

"Sure, but I want you to promise me something. Live or die, I want him returned immediately to his family—all right?"

"I'll do everything I can to see to it."

A few hours later, a government physician arrived at the hospital and relieved Steve of his watch. He gathered all blood samples and reports, then ordered Showalter lifted by helicopter to USAMRIID in Frederick, Maryland. Richville Community Hospital staff told Willie's family that he had contracted a rare virus requiring treatment in a

Washington, D.C. area hospital.

Shortly after arriving in Maryland, the miner's heart stopped beating, and a team of forensic pathologists initiated an extensive autopsy.

# CHAPTER 12

When Steve opened his door to leave for work, his friend, Sheriff Mike Stollard, waited at the threshold.

"Steve, I think you'd better get Alan on the line. We've got one hell of a mess for him to help cover up—"

"What's happened?"

"We got a call this morning from Chester Fife's mother. Two nights ago, he left to visit his girlfriend, and she hadn't seen him since. I went over to Bertha's house about five this morning, and it wasn't pretty. Someone had smashed through the bedroom window and jumped her in her bed. Stabbed her right through the neck."

"Knifed?"

"I doubt it. Four separate marks in the front, a couple passed clear through and into the wall behind the bed. Very little blood on the scene. I'm betting the autopsy will show her body's been drained of blood—"

"Just like Reverend Vance's wife," Steve said.

"Exactly."

"What about the boy?"

"We found his shoes and shirt on the bedroom floor. His car was parked outside the house, but no sign of him.

Some neighbors are out searching the woods, but I don't have a good feeling about how we'll find him."

"One of those things, a female, was on the job site yesterday," Steve said. "It did something to one of my men, Willie Showalter. It was flying away with him when I drove up."

"You mean those things can lift a person?"

"Yeah, with some difficulty. It dropped him and flew away."

"How is he?"

"Not good. When I left, he was in a coma. Alan flew in a special doctor last night. I didn't get in bed until after three."

"It was one hell of a night," Mike said.

"And probably going to get a lot worse before it gets any better." Steve said.

# CHAPTER 13

James Elliott squinted as the morning sun shined past the courthouse wall and into the front seat of his battered old sedan. He wiped the sleep from his eyes, then reached down to the floorboard and fumbled through a pile of empty fast food bags and beer cans. No beer for breakfast. He'd have to make a stop at the convenience store.

A car pulled up alongside his.

"Morning, Sheriff Mike," he said.

"Morning, James," the sheriff said. "It's time you moved your car, unless you have some business to take care of."

The sheriff knew he didn't. James had been parking here almost every night for years. The old car was an eyesore, but as long as it was removed before the start of the work day, the sheriff didn't mind. The street light on the corner of the courthouse afforded a measure of security for the town's best known drunk.

James smiled appreciably, turned the key, saluted the sheriff, and drove to the nearest grocery.

By the time he completed his morning drive, James had finished his liquid breakfast. He parked his car on the mountaintop overlook and tossed the last empty beer can from his six-pack over the guardrail. He belched as he gazed down at a small group of houses nestled in the valley below, then reached in his shirt pocket and pulled out a pack of cigarettes and a lighter. After lighting up, he unzipped his pants and relieved himself over the guardrail.

Hell of a life, he thought. No nagging wife to listen to, no clocks to punch, and money left over from my disability check.

For the past ten years, after abandoning his wife and three step-children one night in a neighboring town, James had been the undisputed town drunk. He mostly lived out of his car, but on really cold nights he'd get himself arrested on a drunk and disorderly to get thrown into the nice, warm town jail. He watched the steam rise from his urine stream, and pondered what hijinks he could pull this winter to get the sheriff's attention.

Before he could zip his pants, something struck him in the shoulder and sent him tumbling head first down the mountain. He rolled for a short distance, then struck his head solidly against the trunk of a tree.

As he slipped into unconsciousness, he felt a stinging at the base of his spine. Then, just before passing into eternal darkness, he heard the pounding of massive wings and felt himself being lifted skyward.

Early the next day, the sheriff's deputy saw James' car parked along the roadside, but since the overlook had always been one of the drunk's favorite haunts, he thought nothing of it.

It wasn't until after he had seen driven past the car again at noon on the next day that he decided to investigate. There were marks in the earth where James had fallen over the guardrail, but no blood or signs of a struggle. The sheriff organized a search party to comb the woods for the missing man. They looked all day before abandoning the search. With temperatures dropping into the teens for the past two nights, everyone assumed James had died from exposure—that was, if he hadn't fallen victim to foul play.

# CHAPTER 14

Two days after Willie Showalter was stung by the female emergent, Steve received a call at his home from Donna.

"Have you heard the news?" she said.

"What news?"

"About your friend, Mr. Showalter. I'd assumed your brother had called you . . ."

"No, Alan only tells me on a need-to-know basis. Willie didn't make it, did he?"

"No. He died yesterday, a little after he was brought to USAMRIID. If it's any consolation, he didn't die in vain. The blood samples we took before he passed away are already telling us a great deal. His body is continuing to educate us. A team of molecular biologists is working around the clock on this case."

"What have they found so far?" Steve scribbled Willie's name on a notepad in pencil and compulsively drew a series of circles around the name.

"They've isolated an enzyme in Mr. Showalter's bloodstream; it appears he did die as a result of a slow-acting sting. Tracing the enzyme to its strongest concentration helped us locate the emergent's egg."

"You mean that thing laid an egg in Willie?"

"Yes, right after it injected him with a combination paralysis/poison. I'd love to get a look at the creature's ovipositor . . ."

"You guys removed the egg already, right? I don't want him coming back next year . . ."

"Not yet—"

"Alan promised me he would return Willie to his family as soon as possible. I assume that the egg will be extracted before then," Steve said.

"I would guess that will still be a few weeks from now."

"Why so long?"

"We're monitoring the changes that are taking place within his body and in the egg. We've already learned that the cells within the egg activated soon after Mr. Showalter passed. It's too early to state with certainty, but it appears my theory about the sustained high levels of lactic acid in the body after death triggering growth in the alien egg may be correct. Finally, after over a year of studying the preacher's carcass, we have an opportunity to gain important insights into the mechanism by which these things transform the human body—"

"Forgive me if I'm less than thrilled, Doctor McKenzie, but that man was a friend of mine. His family hasn't been told, I assume?"

"No, and won't be for the foreseeable future. I'm sorry, Steve. I don't mean to sound cold, but this thing is bigger than any single life. Mr. Showalter's going to provide us with a wealth of information. We've found that the alien's poison, in addition to paralyzing its victim, also acts as a preservative for the host body's cells. It doesn't prevent them from dying, mind you, but it greatly reduces the rate of decay. Are you familiar with what happens to the human body just after death?"

"No, I've always found the subject too depressing . . ." Steve wadded the scrap of paper with Willie's name into a ball and dropped it into his kitchen trash can.

"Bacteria in the intestines start multiplying like crazy after death, and begin the decomposition process. The blood and intestines are attacked first, then gas forms, which leads the intestines to rupture and spread the bacteria to the other organs. That's why it's so important to embalm the dead as soon as possible. Of course, we aren't doing that with Mr. Showalter, and we haven't needed to. The bacteria have somehow been held in check by the preservative in the sting—"

"And the fact that Willie's heart kept beating for hours helped spread the preservative throughout his body," Steve said.

"Precisely. The team's latest theory is that the cells will be preserved from decay long enough for the egg to grow on the nutrients."

"But you guys are going to yank out the egg before it turns Willie's innards to mush—"

"That will be up to someone else. Alan or who, I don't know. The most exciting thing is that we may be able to detect the egg in people who are walking around today with the eggs in them—by looking for the enzyme that the egg gives off while it's waiting for its host to die. It was present in minute levels before Mr. Showalter died. We anticipate it to be similarly detectable in anyone else who has an egg within them."

"But you don't know how it got into those other people, or where. You're not proposing to test millions of people?"

"Of course not, but we hope to narrow it down."

"How? By testing everyone down here? This is the only place where those things have showed up, right?"

"Until today. Alan is shipping a deceased female emergent in to us from rural Michigan. He's identified the human host, and a team of agents will be interviewing everyone who knew the woman to see if there's a connection to your region."

"I hope they put something together soon. At the present rate, there's not going to be anybody left alive down here."

"What do you mean?"

"We've had two deaths and a disappearance in the past three days."

"The emergents?" Donna said.

"How do we know it's plural?"

"At least two, for sure. Showalter was stung by a female and implanted with a fertilized egg. A male and female probably feasted before mating."

"The Sheriff found a young woman dead in her bedroom; all her blood had been drained, just as Mrs. Vance's had been. A few hours later, they found her boyfriend dead in the woods; his blood was drained, too. All this happened the night before Willie was attacked. Two days later, the town drunk disappeared without a trace—"

"He's been stung, too," Donna said.

"How can you be so sure?"

"It all fits the insect reproduction scenario. The first two victims' blood fed the hungry emergents; they needed protein for their bodies prior to attempting fertilization of her eggs. Your friend was stung and injected with a fertilized egg, but losing the host, she was uncertain of that egg's future. The town drunk got her next egg. My guess is the victim is cooling his heels in a hole somewhere."

"In a hole?"

"The host will have to be placed in a dry, sheltered environment to help preserve the body. Some species of wasps dig a hole into the earth and form a cool, dry burial chamber for their egg's host. With its claws, the emergent could easily dig a deep hole, or take advantage of an existing chamber, like a cave or a storm drain."

"We don't have any caves I know of, but there are lots of underground mines—"

"Even a deep cavity under a rock ledge may suffice."

"Great. Needle in a haystack time. How many 'hosts' do you think this thing will lay its eggs in before it dies and ends up a carcass like the Preacher Vance emergent that we found?"

"I can only guess, but I'd say, not many. The female has to expend a great deal of energy getting a heavy adult human into a secure area. But even if there's only one egg-carrying host, you've got three dead humans getting to that point."

"Three?" Steve said.

"Two for the pre-sex meal, and one to lay the egg in. Remember that it's not the quantity of eggs that an insect lays; rather, it's the egg survival rate that counts. If we can't find the human host bodies, that survival rate will be extremely high."

"No wonder the Pentagon wants to exploit this thing, but if something isn't done, this "secret weapon" is going to blow up here on home soil. There's another scary aspect to this. Remember that the preacher emergent returned to his host's home for its meal? It could be a crazy coincidence, but it appears that the emergents return home again. The sheriff found holes in two graves this afternoon—get this—the graves of a husband and wife who died on the same day last year; the husband killed his wife and then himself."

"Synchronous emergence from the grave finally made mating possible," Donna said.

"There's more—the victim and her boyfriend were occupying the home owned by the deceased couple."

"If this isn't just chance, it could mean that the egg passes on some sort of genetic memory, or responds to the earth's magnetic fields," Donna said. "That's beyond belief for me."

"Wouldn't you have said the same about the existence of the emergents in the first place?"

"Touché. Genetic memory or not, the situation's just gotten a lot more interesting . . ."

# CHAPTER 15

One week later, the phone rang in Agent Alan Smith's Washington office.

"Alan, I think we've finished up here in Michigan."

"Jerry, I take it you've got some good news for me?"

"We've found our connection to your hometown. We interviewed the dead woman's husband a second time. This time, one of his sons was present to refresh his memory. It appears the family visited some relatives who lived in the Richville area about five years ago. The relatives moved frequently, so the father had forgotten about it, but the son distinctly remembered going on his first fishing trip on that visit. He said he and an uncle fished at someplace called Big Tumbling Creek . . ."

"Trout stream. I know it well. Does he remember the approximate date?"

"Opening day of fishing season, whenever that was. He said the stream had just been stocked. He caught ten fish his first time out."

"Before you men head home, I want you to get every immediate family member into a clinic for a blood sample," Alan said.

"What do you want us to tell them?"

"Say we suspect some type of slow acting contaminant was in the fish, and we have to have the sample to know for certain."

"Will do, Alan. We'll see you tomorrow in the office."

Agent Smith replaced the receiver, then pulled a file from his top desk drawer and spread the contents on the desktop. He skimmed through the many interviews that had been conducted with friends and relatives of the Reverend Vance and James and Mona Evans.

One note listed fishing as a pastime for Reverend Vance, but did not mention where or when he had fished. Hundreds of locals had traditionally fished at Big Tumbling Creek on opening day—his brother, Steve among them—but it was too early to draw any conclusions. First, it would be necessary to evaluate the blood samples from Michigan for the alien enzyme. If any samples were positive, it would be time to test his hometown fishermen.

# CHAPTER 16

"Steve, it's Donna. I hope I'm not calling too early, but I wanted to reach you before you left for work."

Steve rubbed his eyes and glanced at the digital clock by his bedside——five am.

"I usually get up at six——"

"Oh, I'm so sorry."

"Don't be. What can I do for you?"

"Could you pick me up at the airport about seven this evening? I need to collect some fish and water samples down there."

"You guys had a breakthrough?" Steve said.

"Maybe. I'll have a better idea after I get some samples analyzed."

"We'll get them, then. I'll see you at seven."

"Steve?"

"Yeah?"

"You're a sweetheart, you know that?"

"Yeah, that's what all the cute entomologists tell me. Have a good flight."

The workday passed agonizingly slowly for Steve on the mine site as he waited for evening to arrive. He was anxious to see Donna again, more than he liked to admit to himself. He had never known a woman like her, one complete in herself and her career, and he wasn't sure how to proceed with a relationship, if one were even possible. He was anchored here in his hometown, while she was willing to travel anywhere in the world in search of exotic insects.

For all he knew, the world might be on the verge of an alien invasion, but Donna had already conquered his heart, and all other concerns paled in comparison.

When Donna stepped off the plane, Steve resisted the urge to rush out to greet her on the tarmac, but couldn't stifle the grin on his face as she strolled through the terminal.

"Good to see you again, Steve."

"You, too," he said, taking her bags. He placed her luggage in the back of his SUV and opened the passenger door for her.

"Did they feed you on the plane?"

"Just a pack of peanuts."

"There's a box of granola bars in the glove box to tide you over, then salad and spaghetti at my place—if you're interested?"

"Sounds terrific. And garlic bread?"

"We'll pick up some. Now, what's with these fish and water samples?"

"The agents Alan assigned to the case up in Michigan found one connection to this area. It seems the female host for that emergent had visited with her family down here about five years ago. The son went fishing and caught several from a trout stream called Big Tumbling Creek. Ever hear of it?"

"I'm there every opening day of fishing season. Been going since I was a kid. You don't think these alien eggs got into the trout somehow?"

"I don't know. The stream and fish samples will show me if anything is still present in the waters out there."

"But it won't tell you anything about what might have been there back then . . ."

"No. That's why we need to do selective blood testing."

"To look for that enzyme that your doctors found in Willie Showalter after he was stung?"

"Yes. Steve—would you let me draw a sample of your blood before I leave?"

He didn't say anything, just kept his gaze on the highway.

"I mean, you do always eat the fish you catch?"

"Yeah, most of it. If I have a big catch, I give some of it away to family and friends."

"So, you'll let me?"

"Draw blood? Sure. I don't want to be coming back hurting my neighbors after I finally kick the bucket. How long will it take to get the results?"

"About a week. How will you feel—if the results come back positive?"

"I don't know. Maybe not so bad—if you can promise me it can be removed before it has a chance to start eating my dead flesh."

"Delicate way to put it, Steve." She laughed. "If there's one inside you, we'll find some way to remove it. Hopefully, we will find a way in the future to deactivate or kill the egg with an injection or pill. I hope I'm not depressing you—"

"No, I'm a big boy. What has to be has to be." He reached across the console and gave Donna a quick pat on the knee. "What kind of salad dressing do you like?"

"So, what did you think? Was it edible?" Steve watched

Donna wipe the last traces of spaghetti sauce from the corners of her mouth.

"Excellent. I'd gladly eat leftovers tomorrow."

"Careful, I may make you follow through. How long will you be here?"

"A couple of days."

"You're probably tired from the trip. I assume you'll be my guest for the duration . . ."

"If you'll have me."

"I'll bring your bags in."

While Steve was outside, Donna folded down the covers and removed her shoes.

"Where do you want these?" he said, both arms full of luggage.

"Just put them on the floor."

"I'll grab myself a pillow and blanket from the closet and be out of your hair."

When Steve emerged from the closet, Donna pulled the pillow from his hands and tossed it on the bed.

"We can share," she said. She embraced him and kissed him hungrily. Steve dropped his blanket to the floor and wrapped his arms around her.

# CHAPTER 17

Eight days later, Steve received the call from Donna he had dreaded.

"Steve, how are you?"

"About to die from the suspense. What's the news?"

"Your blood samples were positive for the enzyme. I'm afraid you're carrying one of those eggs inside you."

Steve had told himself he could handle the news, but now, confronted with the reality, he felt himself crumbling inside. "Where do I go from here?"

"You don't have to do anything—just go on with your life as you normally would have. Remember, Steve, there's no evidence the egg and its enzyme are going to have any adverse impact on your life . . ."

"As far as we know. But we don't know a hell of a lot do we? Nothing's happened in the five years since I became a carrier for the egg, but that doesn't mean things can't change tomorrow."

"No, it doesn't. Life's that way for all of us."

"I know. I'm sorry to drag you into my pity party. I'll get this under control."

"I know you will."

"So—how did I get this thing? What did you find in the fish?"

"Nothing. No trace of the egg or enzyme in any fish samples, or the water samples either."

"Then we still don't know where the eggs came from?"

"All that we can state with certainty is that there are no eggs present in the fish or water now. That doesn't mean they weren't present five years ago. The only common thread the agents have found thus far still centers around affected people who fished at Big Tumbling Creek five years ago."

"Does Alan know?"

"No. Thought I'd leave that up to you, if you want to tell him."

"It's better if he knows, right? I mean, the FBI will want to start testing some more of us down here."

"They could, if they build a good enough cover story. Maybe have everyone living in the area come into the health department for testing. But that could cause unwanted media attention. I think it would be easier to take a blood sample after residents die and are brought into the mortuary."

"That would work most of the time," Steve said. "But what about people who've moved out of the area? What about relatives from all over the country who may have eaten those fish during visits to their families?"

"I know. The government is looking at a logistics nightmare for the next few decades. We can only hope the FBI tracking keeps the outbreaks to a minimum, but it's highly unlikely they can keep the presence of these things under wraps. Sooner or later, the world's going to know that we have some dangerous company sharing our planet, and things may never be the same."

# CHAPTER 18

Late May, the following year.

"Mommy, make Jessie give me the camera," Brian said as he tried to yank the disposable snapshot camera from his sister's hands. "She'll cut their heads off."

"Will not," Jessica said, spinning out of her brother's reach. "I want to take Tammy and Roger's picture."

"She's only four years old. That's too young to take pictures," Brian pleaded to his mom.

"Then six is too young, too," Jessica snapped back.

"That's enough out of both of you," their mother said. "Brian, we're going to let Jessie take a couple of pictures, then you can take some."

"Just hurry up, you guys," Tammy said. "We're going to miss the first dance at the prom if we fool around here any longer."

"Eddie'll get us there on time, won't you, Eddie?" Roger asked his older brother, then pulled Tammy closer and smiled for Jessica's first picture.

"No sweat," Eddie said. "We'll get there with time to spare."

"Don't you drive fast," Tammy's mom said. "Her daddy

will have your hide if he hears you've been speeding."

Brian snatched the camera out of his sister's hand as soon as the flash fired for a second time, then started snapping his own pictures.

"Don't you worry none, Mrs. Collins," Eddie said. "I'll get them there and back safe."

"That's enough pictures," Tammy told her little brother. "We've got to be going."

"Tammy, can I have your corsage when you come home?" Jessica said.

"Of course you can, sweetie." Tammy patted her sister on the head as she, Roger, and his brother, Eddie made their way to the car.

Roger opened the door for Tammy, then joined her in the back seat.

"Have a great time," Mrs. Collins said as Eddie revved the engine.

Brian and Jessica stood waving beside their mother as the car disappeared around the first corner of the winding road.

Eddie maneuvered the car down the steep mountain road through a continuous series of curves, occasionally glancing up at his rear view mirror to look at Tammy and Roger in the back seat. His family's mountaintop farm adjoined Tammy's family's farm, and the three had known each other since early childhood.

He was a year older than Tammy and Roger, and like Roger, he had always thought Tammy the prettiest girl he had ever seen. Tammy had been dating Roger for the past two years, and despite the advances of star athletes and the sons of wealthy coal operators, she had eyes only for Roger. Eddie had no doubt that they would wed the summer after high school graduation, but the thought always caused his heart to ache a little. Under different circumstances, he would have asked her to be his girl, but her love for his brother guaranteed that could never be.

About half way down the mountain, Eddie decided to take one more look in the mirror at Tammy—positively radiant in her prom dress. He found himself staring into the mirror for an instant too long and felt the right front wheel drop abruptly off the pavement and onto the low dirt shoulder. Startled, he jerked the wheel back to the left too quickly, and the car shot left into the other lane.

An empty coal truck, taking advantage of a more level stretch of road, had picked up considerable speed, when Eddie's car plowed into its front end. The car was forced back across the other lane and off the narrow mountain road. The vehicle rolled several times down the bare slope, traveling several hundred feet before coming to rest against the abandoned remains of an old coal tipple. All three occupants in the car were declared dead on the scene.

# CHAPTER 19

One year later.

After the death of her sons, Roger and Eddie, Patricia Blevins could no longer bear to live in the home where she had raised her family. She and her husband moved to North Carolina to make a new start; however, they could not bring themselves to sell the property. They left their farm and a dozen head of cattle to the care of a local relative.

Every morning, Patricia's brother, Phil, came to the farm to feed the cattle. In the evenings, he returned to round them up and lock them in the barn for the night.

One evening in late May, shortly after nightfall, the cattle settled into their thick bed of hay on the barn floor. All was quiet, save for the chirping of crickets in the tall clover and the distant sound of a train far away in the valley below. Before midnight, there came the sound of massive wings beating through the air above the barn, but the cattle did not stir.

Three winged creatures flew through the open door in the barn's hay loft and landed without a sound. They folded their wings behind their backs and crawled, as if of a single mind, across the loft floor to a wooden ladder which jutted out of an opening in the center of the loft. One after the other, they crawled head first down the ladder.

Less than twenty four hours prior, these three had emerged from their graves in a nearby cemetery. In tall oak trees that day, they had dried their wings in the sun. Now, it was time for them to feast—in the same barn where their human hosts, Eddie, Roger, and Tammy, had played as children.

Twin, hair lined antennae on the emergents' heads twitched as one by one they reached the ground. The creatures could feel the heat radiating through the blood of cattle scattered across the barn floor. The domestic beasts remained oblivious to the predators in their midst until the emergents sprang like cobras toward three steers.

The surprised cattle jumped to their feet and bawled as the creatures mounted them like bareback riders. The afflicted cattle bucked and tossed about wildly, but they could not dislodge the sharp talons that ripped into their sides. While the other cattle fled to the barn walls, the emergents slashed large arteries in their victims' necks with their claws.

Blood gushed out in streams from the wounds. The emergents' long proboscises rolled out of their mouths, and they feasted like grotesque butterflies on the red nectar that flowed from the dying cattle. One after the other, the emergents rode the steers to the ground as the weakened beasts' knees buckled. For several moments, the demons drank slowly and delicately of the blood.

Their once emaciated stomachs now swollen like bloated ticks, the emergents dismounted their prey and crawled back up the ladder to the loft. They stood before the loft opening, spread their wings, and flew across the pasture fields to the tall trees of the surrounding forest.

Within hours, in an ironic mockery of the lives of their human hosts, the three would mate. Eddie, who had longed for Tammy in life, would now be the first to have her in death, and Roger, who had loved her innocently, would follow in the unholy consummation.

# CHAPTER 20

"Agent Smith, this is Sheriff Stollard in Tazewell County, Virginia."

"Yes, Mike. How are you?"

Even though they had grown up together, Mike felt obligated to address his old friend, Alan, as 'Agent Smith,' but being called by his first name set him at ease.

"Alan, the last time I saw you, you told me to call you if anything further developed down here. Well, two things have happened today."

"I'm listening."

"Early this morning, I got a call from the caretaker for the Klein cemetery. Do you know where that is?"

Agent Smith carried the phone from his desk over to an enlarged topographic map of the Tazewell County/McDowell County region. "Yes, I'm looking at it on a map right now."

"The caretaker said there had been some vandalism done to three graves that I should see. When I arrived at the cemetery, I saw something I'd seen a couple of years ago with Steve.

"The graves of two brothers, Eddie and Roger Blevins,

each had a large circular hole in the grave just in front of the headstones. On the back side of the cemetery, he showed me a similar hole in the grave of a girl named Tammy Collins. I shined my flashlight into each grave; the holes extended all the way through the concrete vaults and into the caskets—just like Preacher Vance's grave back when this all started."

"When did these three individuals die?" Agent Smith said.

"A year ago, about this time. The three, all teenagers, were heading to a prom when they ran into a coal truck and got knocked down the mountain."

"Have there been any creature sightings?"

"No, but something odd happened on the Blevins farm last night."

"If I remember, that would be on the next ridge to the south," Agent Smith said, running his index finger along the contour map just beneath the cemetery symbol.

"That's the place. Since the boys died, the parents have been living in North Carolina. A relative has been tending a few head of cattle for them. Every night, he's been pinning the animals in the barn. This morning, he opened the door and got quite a shock. When he unlocked the door, the cattle came bolting out, all but three, that is. Apparently, something came in through the loft during the night and cut their throats—"

"Cut their throats?"

"Not with a knife or anything like that. There were claw marks on both sides of their necks, and deep gashes into main arteries."

"You think those creatures got them?"

"I'd bet on it. The marks were similar to what I saw when that couple was killed near the old Evans home place. There was a bit of blood, but not near as much as you would expect from such large animals. I believe those things drained as much of the cattle's blood as they needed, then left them there to finish bleeding to death."

"This would be the first time that they've attacked an animal—that we know about. Again, these things have returned to their dead human hosts' stomping grounds to look for their first meal. Maybe they're not that particular about whose blood they drink."

Neither man spoke for a moment, then Agent Smith said, "Did you ask the caretaker and the farmer to keep quiet?"

"I told them not to mention what they'd seen, but you know how that is around here. It'll be hard to keep them quiet for long."

"I'll pay them a visit when I come down." Agent Smith jotted the two men's names down on a notepad on the corner of his desk. "Listen, Mike, I'm going to bring a team down there. Can you meet us at the National Guard Armory in, say, two hours?"

"I'll be there."


Sheriff Stollard checked his watch as a CH-47 Chinook tandem rotor transport helicopter dropped down, right on schedule, on the parking lot at the National Guard Armory. The pilot cut the power to the twin turbines, and the propellers slowed. Agent Smith exited the craft, followed by an Army officer.

Mike greeted Agent Smith and shook his hand. Smith introduced him to the officer, a staff sergeant. While greetings were exchanged, a squad of two fireteams of four soldiers each disembarked from the helicopter. The men unloaded several creates of equipment into two waiting Humvees. Mike watched as the last two crates were loaded into the vehicles.

"Police dogs?" he said.

"Yes," Agent Smith said. "They may be our best shot at capturing live specimens."

"That would be great, as long as we can catch them before they kill someone."

Agent Smith and the sergeant joined Mike in his police cruiser. The two Humvees followed them up ten miles of winding road to the Blevins farm.

Upon arrival, the three vehicles pulled up in front of the barn. The staff sergeant ordered the two canines uncaged, and their handlers led the animals into the barn.

"It stinks in here," the sheriff said as Agent Smith, the officer, and two soldiers entered. "It took a lot of convincing to get the guy to leave this mess here for you."

"We'll see that the carcasses are buried and the blood's cleaned up," Alan said.

The dogs were led up to the three mutilated cattle and allowed to sniff the animals.

"We've got less than an hour of daylight left," Mike said.

"The Blevins house is just down the road," Agent Smith said, "and the girl's family also lives at the end of this road?"

"Correct," Mike said.

"Sergeant, leave one of your teams to clean up the mess here," Agent Smith said. "Follow us with the dogs and the other team."

Agent Smith and the sheriff drove down a gravel road that bisected the pasture fields. In less than a minute, they had driven past the abandoned Blevins house and arrived in the Collins driveway. Mrs. Collins sat on a wooden swing on the front porch. She rose to greet Mike as he got out of the police car.

"Sheriff Stollard, what brings you out on the ridge this

evening?"

"Some wild animals apparently killed some of the Blevins' cattle last night. The National Guard's lending us some men to look for whatever did it. At this point, it appears we may be looking for a pack of wolves."

"Wolves? We've never had any problem with them around here."

"You should stay indoors until we know something further."

"Brian and Jessica are out in the fields with their cousin right now. I'd better run out and tell them."

Mrs. Collins jumped off the porch. Mike gently grasped her arm. "Let me save you the trouble. Where are they?"

"Down by the old corn silo. I never would've let them go out if I'd known."

"I'm sure they're fine. Just wait here, and I'll bring them right back to you."

Mrs. Collins paced the porch as the two vehicles pulled out of her driveway.

# CHAPTER 21

"Amanda, Brian won't pour the tea for me," Jessica said.

"There's nothing in the pot," Brian said. "I'm tired of playing house. This is a dumb old girl's game."

"Ok, Brian," Amanda said. "You don't have to play any more. It's starting to get dark, and your mom's bound to be getting worried. Could you help Jessie gather her toys?"

Fourteen-year-old Amanda Collins watched as the children picked up the pieces of Jessica's plastic tea service from the dry ground in front of the old corn silo. Years ago, this field had been covered each year in corn, but for as long as she could remember, she had played with her older cousin, Tammy, in the tall grass that covered the mountaintop farm's fields.

The silo and the patch of trampled earth around the dilapidated structure resembled a small island in a sea of grass. The field, in turn, was engulfed by the forest. A narrow, well-worn path led from the silo, through the field, and into the trees, where it widened into a winding one lane dirt road. A short distance down the road was the Collins farmhouse.

"Ready, kids?" Amanda said as she started down the path. The children rushed to catch up with her, each grabbing onto one of her hands as they tagged alongside her.

In the year since Tammy's death, Amanda had visited Brian and Jessie as often as possible. They missed their older sister terribly, but Amanda's visits seemed to take their minds off her.

She loved the peaceful beauty of this place. The sinking sun behind their backs cast the field and forest before them in an orange glow. The quarter moon had risen just above the treetops over the point at which the path merged with the forest, like a beacon to guide them home.

"Amy, I see two angels in the sky," Jessica said.

"That's nice, sweetie," Amy said, still gazing at the moon.

"I see them, too!" Brian said.

Amanda looked to the left, and she also saw them. Two thin, masculine, winged shapes descended toward them from over the treetops. Her grip on the children's hands tightened. She wanted to run with them toward the dirt road, away from these impossible apparitions, but she froze. The things flew closer, and Brian said, "It's Roger and Eddie. They've come back from heaven!" The small children yanked free of Amanda's grip and ran toward the descending nude figures.

Amanda's sense of terror intensified, but she could feel her legs again. She wanted to run after the children, save them from these things which could not be, but instead, she bolted toward the nearest part of the forest. Her heart pounded in her throat as she dashed through the waist high grass.

Upon reaching the strands of a barbed-wire fence, she dropped to her stomach and crawled beneath the bottom wire. She rose before clearing the fence; the sharp barbs bit through her blouse and deeply into the flesh of her lower back. She felt the wetness of her blood trickle down into the waist of her jeans, but did not stop to acknowledge the burning pain. She bolted upright and headed toward the forest.

Only after passing the first tall oak tree did she feel safe enough to look back. In the distance, she could make out the children's heads over the top of the tall grass. The larger of the two things stood close to them, and appeared to be gesturing for the other creature to get away. Then, the larger creature apparently knocked the children down, and for about a moment, all she could see was the smaller creature. Suddenly, the large one took to the air. In each hand it grasped a child. It held each child's limp body by the back of their pants and flew into the sky with them.

The other being also took flight, but this one headed straight toward her position across the field. The rays of the setting sun caught in the blazing red eyes of the thing that swooped toward her. She turned and ran for her life through the woods.

# CHAPTER 22

When the sheriff's cruiser and the military vehicle emerged from the forest into the field, there was no sign of the three children. The vehicles pulled up to the bare ground that encircled the cinder block corn silo. Sheriff Stollard and Agent Smith examined the earth in front of the structure.

"They've been here," Mike said, pointing to drawings the children had scratched into the soil.

"Fan out around the area," the sergeant said.

In a few moments, a soldier said, "We've found something over here." He pointed to the pieces of a plastic tea service which had been dropped along the path.

"I don't like the looks of this," Mike said.

"Me either," Agent Smith said.

The sergeant ordered the dogs released from their cages in the back of a Humvee. The dogs sniffed about the toy dishes and followed the alien creatures' distinctive odor in a small circle near the worn foot path.

They sniffed the air, but finding no additional creature scent, directed their attention to Amanda's smell. They ran across the field, following the trail through the tall grass, beneath the barbed wire fence, and into the adjacent forest. The dogs' handlers chased after them. Soon, the two soldiers had disappeared with the dogs into the woods.

# CHAPTER 23

Amanda knew that the thing would be unable to fly into the woods after her, but she suspected it would be able to chase her on the ground. There was little chance she could outrun it for long, but perhaps it would not be necessary to keep running. Having played here with her cousin, Tammy, since childhood, she knew these hills well.

She knew that about a third of the way down the mountain, there was a narrow opening in a rock cliff. This opening led to a series of shallow caves that crisscrossed under the mountain. She had played in them with Tammy, Roger, and Eddie on numerous occasions, but they had always carried flashlights, and the boys' sense of direction had always seemed to help them find their way back outside into the daylight . . .

Daylight. So precious little left now, and the heavy forest canopy hastened the darkness. Amanda could hardly see the trees before her, but she thought she could make out the light colored sandstone rock cliff just ahead.

She quickened her pace down the hill, and did not see a long, dead tree limb jutting from the forest floor just ahead. The limb caught in the leg of her jeans, and her forward momentum pitched her up into the air like a pole vaulter and hurled her down the steep slope.

The breath was knocked out of her, but there were no broken bones. She shook her head, jumped to her feet, and continued toward the light colored shape ahead.

She experienced a brief sense of relief when she reached out and touched the sandstone rock cliff. She proceeded carefully along a narrow ledge in the rock outcropping, feeling in the dark for the narrow vertical opening in between the rocks that could offer her sanctuary.

Finally, her right hand pushed out into emptiness; she had found the opening. She squatted on the rock ledge before the keyhole shaped opening, the very top of which wasn't much wider than her open hand. She held onto the opening's sides and pulled herself in.

She leaned back against a stone wall and allowed herself a moment to gasp for air. Would the creature be able to find her here? If it did, the caves would offer no protection. She would be trapped like a rat in a barrel, waiting for her executioner to come in after her.

There was another cave opening—one that lead outside—somewhere on the opposite side of the mountain. The boys had taken her and Tammy out that way once, but it had been a long, scary crawl, and there were many twists and turns that only the boys would remember. The boys—they were dead now, and something that looked like one of them was somewhere outside the cave searching for her.

There was another option—if the crow bar were still there—and if she had the strength to do with it what the boys had told her could be done . . .

The emergent which had once been Roger Blevins neared the rock cliff. It had not seen Amanda since she ran into the forest, but with its acute sense of smell, it did not need to. The young girl's body had released a continuous stream of human pheromone as she rushed down the mountain, leaving an invisible trail which registered in the setae of the creature's antenna and guided it unerringly to the cave mouth.

Amanda had always liked Eddie and Roger, but they both had a mean streak. Once, before they had showed the girls the second cave opening, the boys teased Amanda and Tammy that they were going to seal themselves inside the cave with the girls.

The boys had left a crow bar just inside the entrance, and threatened to use it to pry loose a large slab of stone perched precariously over the entrance. Roger had held onto each girl as his brother slid the crow bar into the crack above the slab and started pulling down.

The stone had groaned from the strain, and Eddie stopped immediately, scaring himself with the realization that he really could bring the stone down. He tried to pull the bar back out, but it was stuck, and he feared that trying to free it would dislodge the slab.

On numerous future visits, the boys had jokingly asked the girls, "Do you want to bring the house down?" But they had never reached for the bar again.

Amanda's pulse and respiration rate had slowed considerably. She listened for sound outside the cave. Crickets, an owl hooting in the distance, and then—the snap of dry twigs somewhere outside.

The time had come to make a decision. If the thing was out there, it would easily make it inside. There was only one choice; she groped in the darkness over her head, and there it was, jutting out from the crack over the entrance—the cold steel crow bar.

She reached up with both hands and started pulling

down with all her might. There came a groaning sound, as there had been years before, then, without further protest, the massive layer of rock came crashing down to the cave floor, sealing the entrance. The ground shook with the impact, and a sudden gust of wind from the falling rock blew onto her sweat-soaked face.

The reverberation from the fall soon subsided, and all was quiet in the cave. Then, there came a loud scratching sound from the other side of the stone slab that blocked the entrance.

There's no way he can get through that mess, she thought. She expected him to give up quickly, but the furious scratching continued for several minutes, until she heard dogs barking outside.

# CHAPTER 24

The German shepherds rapidly made up the distance between themselves and their quarry. When the first dog came upon the emergent, it was busy scraping at the stone which blocked the entry to the cave. The dog raced across the narrow ledge and bit deeply into one of the creature's wings.

The emergent spun around angrily and swatted at the dog. One of its razor sharp talons struck the dog in the chest. The impact knocked the dog backwards off the ledge, but not before it tore a foot long section out of the emergent's wing. The wounded dog yelped in pain as it tumbled down the slope.

The soldiers approached the cliff and trained their flashlights in the injured dog's direction. The second dog growled as it approached the emergent from the opposite side. The alien creature heard the men approaching and decided to retreat straight back up the mountain.

The dog pursued, but the alien easily outdistanced it. The beam of one of the soldier's flashlights fell for an instant upon the creature's glowing red eyes as it tore through the underbrush mere yards away.

"What the hell was that?" the soldier said.

"I don't think we want to know," the other answered. He pulled a portable radio from his back pack. "Sergeant, this is alpha team. Something's headed your way. It's taken out one of the dogs, and it doesn't look happy."

"Roger," the sergeant said. "We've got bravo team and the rest of alpha waiting up here for it."

Less than two minutes later, the creature had made its way to the clearing. The sun had set, but without the heavy forest canopy, the soldiers on the mountaintop could still see across the field. The emergent saw the soldiers waiting along the barbed wire fence and avoided them by climbing up the trunk of a dead poplar tree.

It crawled out on a limb and leaped out into the air, but the damage to its wing was severe. It tumbled like a broken butterfly to the ground, but recovered with feline grace and darted through the tall grass, heading toward the corn silo.

One soldier stood directly in the creature's path, but it did not turn away; instead, it charged straight toward him.

He pulled his pistol from its holster and emptied the clip into the beast; it twitched with the impact of each bullet, but kept coming.

As soon as the last round exited the barrel, the emergent was upon him. It plunged its talons deep into the soldier's chest, then yanked them out like a withdrawn sword. The man fell dead at his slayer's feet. It bounded over his body and headed straight for the opening at the bottom of the silo.

Several soldiers fired in vain at the creature as it dived into the silo's access door.

"We've got it now," Agent Smith said to the sergeant.

"How do you propose we coax it out of there?" the officer said. "Offer it a steak and throw a net over it when it comes out?"

"I don't care how you bring it out—as long as it comes out alive," Smith said.

"You'll take it how you can get it," the sergeant said.

"That's not what the Pentagon ordered," Smith said.

"Orders be damned," the sergeant said. "Did you just see what that thing did to my soldier? I'm not risking another man's life to capture your trophy." He turned away from the FBI agent, toward his troops. "Alpha team, get out the bazooka. Load a concussion rocket and fire into the silo door."

One soldier retrieved a case from the back of a Humvee and snapped open the lid. Within seconds, the weapon was loaded and ready. The soldier dropped to one knee with the bazooka over his shoulder and took careful aim.

"Fire!" the sergeant ordered.

The rocket entered the open silo door. A loud boom, then a cloud of dust as the decrepit cinder block and mortar structure caved in. In an instant, the silo was reduced to a pile of rubble.

"What now?" Agent Smith said to the sergeant.

"We wait for a couple of minutes for signs of life, and if we don't hear any, we start digging the damned thing out," the officer said.

After nearly five minutes of silence, the sergeant ordered the four men of bravo team to start removing the rubble by the Humvee headlights. The sergeant and the remaining member of alpha team stood close by with their rifles at the ready, in the event that the creature had survived the explosion.

While Agent Smith and the sergeant stood by watching the silo excavation, the voice of one of the dog handlers came over a portable radio in the front seat of a Humvee.

"Sergeant, we've got a girl trapped down here in a cave.

Apparently, that thing was trying to dig its way in after her when the dogs jumped him."

"How many?" Sheriff Stollard said. "There were three children out here."

"Is there more than one person in the cave?" the sergeant said.

"Let me check," the sergeant replied. He asked the other dog handler, and the man shouted the question into the rock pile blocking the cave entrance. He strained to hear the reply from within.

"She's the only one in there," the other soldier relayed to the sergeant.

"What's her name?" the sheriff said.

"Amanda," came the reply.

"God," Sheriff Stollard said. "Something's happened to the little ones."

"What are you going to need to get her out?" the sergeant said.

"A jack hammer, picks, shovels for starters," the sergeant said.

"I'll contact Steve," the sheriff said. "He can supply us with the tools and a compressor for the jackhammer." Mike turned away from the officer, toward Alan. "Agent Smith, I'm going to stop to talk with Mrs. Collins for a minute on the way out."

"What are you going to tell her?" Smith said.

"That we think the kids are trapped in the cave—anything but the truth, I guess," Mike said.

Agent Smith nodded his consent. That would buy them some time, but if word got out about children being trapped, the neighbors would come from miles around to offer their assistance. "Tell her we're going to take care of this, that we don't need anyone else coming around; they'd just get in the way."

"I'll do my best," the sheriff said. He got into his cruiser and drove toward the Collins home.

After an hour of excavating, the emergent was uncovered. The pale grey being lay motionless in a fetal position on the crumbled silo's concrete slab floor. Its bright red eyes were open and stared straight ahead toward the soldiers' boots.

"Doesn't look like your bug made it," the sergeant said to Agent Smith.

"Don't be so sure," Smith said. "It looks pretty good, considering what happened to it. There are no visible wounds—no blood anywhere."

"What's the damned thing made of—rubber?" the sergeant said.

"For his sake and yours, we'd better hope so, sergeant," Smith said. "I want him bundled up tight, pronto. Get the chopper pilot on the radio. I want him up here in the next ten minutes."

The soldiers removed another case from a Humvee. This one contained an assortment of chains and neck, ankle, and wrist bracelets, along with four metal bars—one to immobilize each limb. All the restraints and chains were composed of a light weight, stronger than steel, alloy.

At first, the two men assigned the task of securing the creature hesitated to come near it, and the rifles trained upon its still body offered little sense of security. They had seen what this thing had done to a member of their squad, and they feared that any moment, it would spring to life and slay them as it had their friend.

The first soldier touched one of its feet cautiously, then, gaining his nerve, he reached out for the other foot. His assistant reached out for the creature's wrists, careful to avoid the long, razor sharp claws that extended from each finger. The talons of one hand were still covered with the fallen soldier's dried blood.

"Bring him over in the grass and stretch him out on his back, boys," Agent Smith said.

The soldiers found the creature to be of surprisingly light weight. They carried it by its chains hands and feet to a batch of grass next to the open box of and restraints. Here, they easily straightened its arms and legs, placing the extended arms along either side of the sunken torso. They attached the neck, wrist, and ankle shackles, then snapped the long metal arm and leg bars into locking notches in the shackles. A chain was threaded through a loop in the opposite end of each metal bar.

The men worked quickly, wrapping additional chains in a crisscross pattern around the front and back of the body.

The three remaining members of alpha team sealed the gore stained body of their fallen comrade in a body bag. Their sad deed completed, they tenderly placed his remains in the back of a Humvee.

By the time they had completed their task, the huge CH-47 Chinook transport helicopter dropped down onto the field.

"Load it carefully, boys," Agent Smith said. "We've got a special room waiting for this fellow."

The soldiers looked to the sergeant for confirmation. He nodded his approval, and ordered the men to accompany the creature on its journey to USAMRIID in Maryland.

"I'll ride with it to the lab," Agent Smith told the sergeant. "Keep working on getting that girl out of the cave. I'll have one of my agents in here to interview her as soon as you pull her out."

# CHAPTER 25

In transit, Agent Smith phoned Dr. McKenzie at home to tell her of the creature's capture. Minutes later, she waited near the landing pad for the helicopter to touch down at USAMRIID.

The creature was still stunned from the concussion grenade and the weight of thousands of pounds of rubble which had collapsed upon it.

After carrying the emergent into a titanium lined vault, the soldiers unlocked the chains which had bound its limbs, then bolted the door shut. Agent Smith accompanied Donna to the new lab's control center. She switched on the video cameras and waited for signs of movement.

"Do you think it's still alive?" Smith said.

"It shouldn't be, but I suspect that it is."

"Can't you hook it up to some electrodes, or listen for a heartbeat or something?"

"Do you want to borrow my stethoscope and go in there to check?" Donna said.

"No."

"Me either. Let's just sit here and wait to see what happens."

Agent Smith paced the floor for nearly an hour before there came a sign of life. The creature's limbs twitched slightly. Then, it stood upright slowly, extending its wings as if to take flight. It carefully surveyed its prison, testing each wall with its claws for the slightest opening.

After circling the room several times, it grew agitated and attempted to fly toward the ceiling, but the damaged inflicted upon its wings by the police dog and the falling debris was severe. It leaped repeatedly toward the grill-covered lights in the ceiling, each time slamming into the ceiling with such force that Donna feared it would manage to shatter the high intensity lamps and plunge the chamber into darkness.

She turned off all the lights in the room. A few moments later, after the lamps had cooled, the noises in the chamber stopped. The creature had, for the moment, accepted the futility of its situation and ceased its frantic activity.

"How did you know that would work?" Smith said.

"I didn't, but it worked with a bumble bee that was trapped in a classroom one night, so I thought it worth a shot." Donna said. "Speaking of shot, I'm going to call it a night. You coming out?"

"Yeah," Agent Smith said.

Donna bid him goodnight, locked up the lab, and headed home for some rest.

# CHAPTER 26

Agent Smith scooped up the ringing phone from his desk and carried a stack of folders to his filing cabinet.

"Smith speaking," he said. He rested the phone in the crook of his neck and pulled open the cabinet's top drawer.

"Alan, it's Steve."

"Steve, what's up?"

"You heard they got Amanda out of the cave early this morning?"

"Yes, one of my agents is talking to her at the hospital. I understand she's going to be fine."

"As well as a kid can be after what she's been through. She blames herself for what happened to the little kids. You know people around here are going to think she's lost her mind if she tells them what she saw."

"That's why we're going to encourage her to let us help her with her story," Alan said.

The cover-up, while essential, nevertheless disgusted Steve. "Listen, I'm standing outside on a reclaimed underground mine bench. Do you remember the old Tiller mine?"

"Vaguely. Didn't we have some relative who worked

that mine before it shut down?"

"Yeah, Uncle Wilson. Do you remember it well enough to find it from the air?"

"I think so. Have you found something?"

"Looks like I've stumbled upon the nest for the things that took those little kids," Steve said.

"You've seen one of the creatures again?"

"No, but I've got good reason to believe that I'm looking at one of their entrance holes. I was out here to check the pH on the discharge water from the old mine. When I drove up to the sealed entry, I noticed a smooth circular hole just to the right of the wall of cinder blocks used to seal the mine."

"Not an auger hole?"

"Too small and too fresh. I'd know if anyone had been down in here with heavy equipment. Nothing bigger than my Jeep has been down this road for years. No, this hole is just like the ones we've found in the tops of the graves those things have clawed their way out of—only this time, the hole extends horizontally into the mountain."

"Can you open the mine up for me?" Alan said.

"Sure, I can get a dozer trammed over here in a couple of hours from the strip site, but there's state and federal notifications to be made before reopening the mine—"

"I'll take full responsibility for the shortcuts. What will we be looking at, if we have to crawl back in there?"

"The mine's been sealed for over twenty years. The pillars were pulled during retreat mining, which means that the intake and exhaust air entries are the only two corridors left open. Given all the shifting and roof falls that have occurred, it may be impossible to even crawl back through there. A considerable stream of water comes from the discharge pipe in the mine seal year round, but not so much that we'd have a dam burst situation or anything like that if we knock out the seal."

"How about gas?"

"If I remember our uncle's stories, this was one gassy mine. The air intake fan hasn't worked for years, so the whole thing's probably filled with methane."

"Go ahead and get that bulldozer," Agent Smith said. "I should be there in a couple of hours."

"Will do. See you in a few."

# CHAPTER 27

Steve had a small bulldozer unloaded on the site within an hour and a half. Just as the bulldozer's blade knocked down the cinder blocks which formed the mine seal, Steve heard a helicopter, then saw a green, camouflage colored Bell Jet Ranger drop over the mountaintop. The pilot, with great precision, dropped the craft down onto the narrow mine bench just beyond where the bulldozer was working.

A couple of minutes later, Steve's brother Alan and another man, both clad in coveralls, emerged from the helicopter and joined Steve beside his Jeep.

"Steve, I'd like you to meet Special Agent Jerry Connor. He was involved in the emergent body recovery up in Michigan."

Steve extended his hand. "Good to meet another member of the club. It's hard for anyone to believe in these things until they've seen one up close."

"I've never seen a live one, so you're one up on me," Agent Connor said.

"Just stick around, and you might get your chance," Steve said. "We've got two emergents unaccounted for, and two little kids who we suspect they've dragged in there."

The three men watched as the bulldozer raised its wide blade high for the final time, dropped it down to the ground in front of the remaining debris, then backed away from the mine entrance with the remnants of cinder blocks, mortar, and earth in tow on the blade's back side.

Steve signaled the dozer operator to shut down his engine. He jumped up on the bulldozer's tracks and opened the operator's cab door.

"Tram it on out to the asphalt road, Joe," Steve told the operator. "I'll have them waiting with a low-boy to haul the dozer and you back to the strip site."

"Who are those boys in the whirlybird?" Joe said.

"Just a couple of federal mine inspectors," Steve said. "They'll chew the company's ass out over the iron content in our discharge or some such."

"Ok, see you on the job," Joe said. He fired up the diesel engine, and Steve closed the cab door and jumped off the tracks. The dozer lurched forward and headed away from the mine site.

The agents waited beside Steve's Jeep.

"Shall we have a look inside, gentlemen?" Steve said. "I have a couple of extra mine caps and lamps in the back seat."

Steve placed a hard shell mine cap on his head, and the other two men watched closely and imitated as he attached the lamp's battery pack around his waist. The men approached the newly exposed mine entrance.

"My main interest is over here," Steve said. "The creatures dug their hole into the mine fill just to the right of the mine seal. Looks like they preferred doing things the hard way. Lord knows their claws could've ground right through those cinder blocks, but they preferred to dig

114

through ten feet or more of backfill. After a ways, as you can see now that the mine seal has been removed, letting some light into the entry, their little tunnel turns to the left, right into the open mine entry, just behind the mine seal."

The agents followed Steve and squatted down to look into the shallow darkness. The cold, damp mine air, nearly thirty degrees cooler than the outside summer air, hit their faces like an autumn breeze. They dropped to their knees and crawled over the smooth, wet slate that formed the mine floor.

"I don't think it's safe to crawl more than a few feet back into here," Steve said. "We'll only have air for a short distance before the methane takes over, and I'm not going to risk passing out with those things possibly hanging out in here."

The men trained their lamps straight ahead, revealing a level entry relatively free of rock or other debris. "We could get a mine scoop back in here with no problems," Steve said. "Of course, we have no way of knowing if there are roof falls just beyond what our lights are showing—"

"What's wrong?" Alan said. "Did you see something?"

"Over there." Steve motioned to the right with his cap light to a spot about twenty feet away. "I thought I saw something white up there, right about where the first crosscut would be between us and the second heading."

"I think I see something, too," Agent Connor said, crawling ahead.

"Jerry," Alan said, "wait up."

Agent Connor ignored Alan and crawled quickly across the mine floor.

"It's a foot!" Connor said.

"One of the kids?" Steve said.

"No, older. A teenager, maybe. Wait, there are wings on its back. It's a female—one of those things. It looks dead."

Steve and Alan arrived beside Agent Connor. The emergent's body lay in a fetal position in a narrow cavity in what had once been the crosscut between mine entries number one and number two. The roof over the cut had caved in during retreat mining decades before.

Steve shined his lamp on the creature's stringy black hair, then upon the bony arms, bent at the elbows, drawn tightly to the torso, hands forward at the wrists resembling a praying mantis waiting to spring toward its prey.

The beam of his head lamp traced down across the blue, translucent insect wings to the emaciated, wasp-thin waist and prominent hip bones, past stick thin legs to the pale, deathly grey feet which had first caught his attention.

Agent Connor reached out cautiously to touch the cold creature's shoulder, then pulled the body toward him to better see its face. The lights of all three men's lanterns met on the dead being's pasty, grey head. Their attention was drawn to the abnormally large, red eyes which shined like highway sign reflectors under their lamps. At the top of the head, directly above each eye, was a long, moth-like antennae.

"This used to be Tammy Collins," Steve said to the men. "She died about this time last year on her prom night. She was engaged to marry one of the boys who was in the car with her. The other boy was her fiancé's older brother."

"He's probably the one we have in USAMRIID," Alan said.

"Where do you think the other one is?" Agent Connor said.

"Maybe lying dead in here somewhere, or in the woods outside," Steve said. "Donna says the females outlive the males after mating. The female's dead, so we shouldn't have anything to fear from her boyfriend."

"But how do we know they've mated?" Jerry said.

"We won't know positively until we find those kids," Alan said. "I'm betting we'll find them somewhere in here. First, we need to bag this specimen. Jerry, grab an ankle, and let's drag it out of here. It doesn't appear she'll be too heavy."

After pulling the body outside, Alan told Agent Connor to obtain a body bag from the helicopter. He returned with a long vinyl sack, and Steve helped them place the stiff creature within.

Alan zipped the bag shut. "Steve, I'm going to fly to USAMRIID with this. I'll bring a federal mine inspector back with me this afternoon. See if you can locate a couple of your company's underground miners who are willing to do a search and rescue into the mine this evening for the children."

"I'll get what we need together," Steve said. "Have a safe flight."

# CHAPTER 28

Dr. McKenzie slept for a few hours, then returned to the federal installation shortly after noon. She was surprised to find two armed military police stationed to either side of the lab entrance, and amused that the base had gone to such extreme security measures. Granted, the creature had put up quite a struggle before capture, and its predecessors had demonstrated the ability to burrow through steel caskets and concrete burial vaults, but there was no chance it could claw its way out of the high security vault adjoining her lab.

The guards glanced at her photo ID, then nodded their consent for her to enter. She slid her plastic identity card into the electronic lock. The lock flashed green; she removed the card and entered the anteroom of her lab. To her surprise, a military officer sat at her desktop computer, and four soldiers stood before the door to her lab.

"What the hell is going on here?" she said.

The man swiveled around in her chair, stood, and offered his hand.

"Dr. McKenzie, I presume?"

Donna refused to shake his hand.

"I'm Major Alexander Stidham. The Pentagon has placed me in charge of this phase of the project."

"No one contacted me—"

"They were under no obligation to do so. However, I'm willing to allow you to remain in an observational capacity until we are finished here."

She wanted to say, "You arrogant bastard," but bit her tongue instead. The Pentagon had been good to her the last couple of years. While on this project, she had enjoyed a break from applying for scientific grants and wondering where the next day would take her. Donna reluctantly nodded her agreement.

"I have read all your notes," Major Stidham said. "Fascinating, thorough work. You've done a fine job. I was a practicing physician before joining the Pentagon—in case you were wondering."

"I wasn't. What's this project phase you're talking about?"

"This is our first opportunity to observe a living specimen. According to your reports, the male of the species has an especially brief life span; therefore, it is essential that we complete our experiment as soon as possible."

"Experiment? What kind of experiment?" Donna said.

"There are things we must learn, such as how strong are these creatures? How do they react when their backs are up against the wall? How do they attack their prey?"

"I'm sure you've read Agent Smith's reports of the emergent's capture?"

"Yes, but we need filmed documentation."

"How do you propose to obtain this footage?"

"Step into the next room with me, and we'll begin."

They passed counters lined with microscopes, beakers, and other lab equipment as they made their way to the far end of the rectangular room, where two technicians were seated before a computer command center.

"Bring the lights up slowly," the major ordered.

Donna looked to the TV monitors located to either side of the technicians at the control center. The screens went from pitch black to bright, revealing the contents of the titanium lined chamber from the ceiling mounted video cameras located in each corner of the room. In the first screen, Donna saw the emergent crouched in one corner of the unfurnished room, facing the walls with its folded, iridescent wings toward the camera.

Another monitor revealed something new and unexpected in the room. A cube, resembling a shark cage, rested along one wall. Donna reached over a technician's shoulders for the camera's controls and zoomed in on the object.

"There's a man in there!" Donna said.

"Yes."

"But why?"

"The man in the cage is a convicted international terrorist, facing several life sentences for a heinous crime against the citizens of one of our nation's allies. He consented to take part in our little experiment."

"I'm sure he did. You've got to get him out of there, right now."

"I assure you he would be terribly disappointed. We promised him the opportunity to fight for his freedom."

"Fight? That thing will rip him to shreds."

"Maybe. Maybe not. We shall see." Major Stidham picked up a stand mounted microphone from the control panel.

"Abdul," he said, "it's time to come out."

They watched on the monitor as the cage top flipped open. A tall, dark skinned man jumped out, wielding a long knife with a serrated blade.

Their attention turned to the monitor showing the emergent. The beast whirled around at the sound of the cage opening; its red eyes glared at the man standing across the room.

"What devil is this?" the man said in broken English. Perspiration dotted his face. He crouched in a fighting stance, with the knife held out before him.

The creature sprang without warning, and with a single bound, it was upon him. The man crashed to the floor, the impact knocking the knife out of his hand.

The heavy knife skidded into the corner, far out of reach. Abdul kicked and tried desperately to push the beast off of him, but it was too strong. It rolled him face down on the floor, then sat upon the small of his back.

Donna stared in disbelief as a long, curved ovipositor/stinger emerged from the base of the creature's spine and stabbed into the man's back. After imbedding in his flesh, the organ convulsed, releasing a potent toxin into Abdul's blood-stream. Almost instantly, he went limp as paralysis overcame his body. Again, the ovipositor convulsed, this time implanting its egg in the man.

The emergent retracted its stinger and crawled off the dying man. It remained close by his side, instinctively guarding the human host of its progeny.

Everyone was momentarily stunned, then the major spoke.

"What just happened here?" Major Stidham said.

"We watched you send a man to his death," Donna said.

"But he didn't die in vain," Stidham said. "We both learned something new, didn't we? According to your reports, only the female is equipped with an ovipositor. We both assumed that because the human host was male, the emergent would be the same sex. A reasonable assumption, since up until now, the sex of all of our previous specimens corresponded to that of their human hosts . . .

"In your absence this morning, Agent Smith delivered the deceased female from Michigan." Stidham pointed to a row of mortuary drawers on an adjoining wall which housed the new arrival's remains and previous emergents. "You might want to begin your autopsy today to see if our live she-male, Roger Blevins, is merely an aberration."

Major Stidham ordered the technicians to turn down the light intensity in the emergent's chamber, removed a flash drive from a computer, and dropped it into an attaché case on the control center counter. The major took one last look at the emergent in the monitor. It still sat quietly beside its victim.

"He's probably still alive, you know," Donna said. "We may be able to save him."

"He's more valuable as a test subject," Stidham said. "We need to know how long this process will take, the stages along the way. I needn't explain to you, of all people." He picked up the attaché case from the counter and started out of the room.

"I'll stop by for your report on the female's autopsy later this week. In the meantime, the guards will remain in place until further notice. Keep up the good work, Dr. McKenzie."

Right, Donna thought.

Stidham strutted out the lab's front door.

She was repulsed by the path the project had taken and the type of man she now found herself allied with. I'm as guilty as he is, by association, she thought, and immediately felt dirty, a kind of spiritual filthiness that nothing could ever cover up or make clean.

# CHAPTER 29

"Those things are going to kill you," Steve said, as Elmer lit up his cigar.

"S'what they told me for 40 years about rock dust," Elmer mumbled around his Cuban. "Ain't got me yet."

Retired for five years after working for forty underground, the square-jawed, barrel-chested man with a snow white crew-cut amazingly still had the physique of an active Marine drill sergeant.

Steve unrolled a large mine map on the hood of his Jeep Cherokee, anchoring the old linen map on one end with a half can of soda and a fist-sized stone on the other. Elmer and Ron, a young mine rescue team member, leaned over the vehicle's fenders for a look at the mine workings. Glen, a federal Mine Health and Safety (MSHA) inspector who flew in with Alan, was beside Steve on the other side of the car hood. Alan stood off to the side, near the mine entry, talking on his cell phone.

"What have we got?" Glen said.

"Five entries, intake air on entry number one, the outside left entry, exhaust on the far right, entry number five," Steve said, pointing on the map to what had once been five separate horizontal tunnels driven into the mountain. "They mined on fifty foot centers between the entries, so that leaves us with 20 foot wide cross-cuts to look into about every thirty feet along the right side of the entry. I expect the top of the three center entries have caved in to the mine floor. They pulled the pillars when they abandoned the mine, what, over 20 years ago, Elmer?"

"Yeah, thereabouts. I think we sealed her up in the summer of 1990."

"From the map, it looks like they removed most of the pillars, so there won't be much depth to the crosscuts," Steve said. "The floor elevation slopes downhill from the face to the outside; we expect that the kids will be found closer to the face, away from the water, so we won't bother to look into the crosscuts until on the way out—if we don't find them at the face, that is. It's about a mile and a half from here at the drift mouth to the face. I figured we'd use a scoop as a mantrip to take us down the intake entry." Steve glanced to Elmer as if to ask his approval.

"We should be able to do that," Elmer said. "We always had good top in there. There may be a lot of water in some low places, though. We may not be able to go all the way to the face without getting the wheels hung up in the mud."

"We should be able to drag the kids out the rest of the way," Steve said. "They won't weigh very much."

"From the looks of things, the seam averages about 36 inches in most places," the federal inspector said after doing a series of quick calculations on a notepad. "That dragging could get mighty tiring when you're crawling on your belly."

"How'd them kids get all way back in that mine?" Ron said. "Wild animal of some kind get them?"

"Yeah, you might say that," Steve said. He hated lying to the men, but Alan told him he had no choice in the matter. They wouldn't have believed him if he had told them, and besides, it wasn't as if they were going to encounter one of the creatures in the mine. The female creature was dead, and its body had already been bagged and sent to USAMRIID.

According to Donna, the male had probably died soon after mating with the female. The female had fulfilled her biological imperative by injecting her eggs into the two missing children. That probably meant the male was dead in the woods somewhere; therefore, with the other male in captivity at USAMRIID, all three "emergents," as Donna liked to refer to them, were accounted for.

Perhaps, Steve reasoned, the fact that the captured male was still alive indicated that he had not mated with the female, and was still clinging onto life a bit longer in anticipation of a mating that would not occur.

"Any questions?" Steve said as he rolled up the mine map. The other three men shook their heads.

"All right then, let's do it," Steve said. "It's about 4 o'clock. With any luck, we'll have them out of there before 6."

The men stood over a battery-powered scoop parked just outside the drift mouth. Ron, the youngest member of the company's mine rescue team, handed each man a closed circuit respirator pack to strap on their backs, and a full face mask that attached via hose to the back pack. "You all know how to use these?" he said.

Elmer and the mine inspector nodded. Steve hesitated for a moment, ashamed to admit that, in spite of his mining degree and nearly ten years of surface mining experience, he had never tried on a respirator.

"I'll . . . need some help with mine," Steve said.

Ron tightened the elastic straps to secure the mask tight against Steve's face. "That ought to do it," he said. "Keep in mind that we've got about 4 hours worth of air in these units, but only 50 minutes if we have to exert ourselves."

"Do you have a gas detection unit?" Steve asked Glen, his voice muffled by the clear plastic facemask.

"Yes," the MSHA inspector said, obviously annoyed. "Right here in my canvas bag."

"We'll need it," Elmer said. "This was always a gassy mine. One spark, and we may all be blown to bits."

Another reason, Steve thought, that we can't carry any type of firearms into the mine. And if one of those creatures waited in there, nothing less than a cannon could offer a man better than a snowball's chance in hell.

"Let's assume the positions," Ron said. He lay on his stomach facing the mantrip's hand controls. Elmer and the mine inspector lay just behind and to the right of the operator in the vehicle bed. Just as Steve prepared to belly down onto the bed, he felt a hand on his shoulder. It was his brother, Alan.

"Steve, you don't have to do this," Alan said. "These men can handle it without you." He noticed Steve's complexion had turned ashen and beads of sweat dotted his forehead.

"This is something I've got to do," Steve said. "I used to date these kids' mother in high school. They could've been mine, you know."

"Yes, I know," Alan said.

Neither spoke of the dream, but they were both aware of it at this moment. On numerous occasions in their childhoods, Steve had spoken of his nightmare, the dream in which his imaginary future self was killed in a mine cave in. Despite the passage of so many years, the dream and the dread of the underground remained vivid, yet ironically, he had settled on a career which regularly led him past underground mine openings.

He had confronted his fears twice in the summer of his junior year in college; a summer job with a large surface mining company with underground mine holdings had required him to go a couple of hundred feet into an unventilated underground mine to write down the serial numbers of some mining equipment.

The other occasion was with a survey crew. They were assigned to run an elevation from inside the mine, and while they were underground, the mountain shook with the terrifying concussion of a routine blast set off to dislodge the coal.

Both times, Steve had felt he would resign his summer job before confronting his fears; now, he found his principles forcing him once again into the bowels of the earth.

Alan realized Steve had demonstrated great courage earlier in the day when they had crawled less than 50 feet into the mine to retrieve the dead creature's body. Now, his brother was about to leave the daylight far behind, and travel perhaps a mile or more into the darkness.

Alan clasped Steve's hand for a moment, then watched him lie flat upon his belly in the mantrip. The battery powered vehicle jerked to a start and disappeared into the mine's black, shallow mouth.

# CHAPTER 30

For the first few hundred feet, Steve hugged the mantrip's steel bed, terrified to look left or right or raise his head the slightest. "Always keep your head down while riding in a mantrip," a voice inside his head kept repeating.

Once, while surveying around the exterior operations area of an underground mine, he had seen a miner whose entire ear had been ripped off of his head years before, simply because the man had failed to keep his head down while entering or exiting the mine. The image of the pink scar tissue where the man's ear had once been still lingered in his mind.

The air temperature, a constant 55 degrees year round, if he remembered his mining textbooks, made him shiver and wish he had worn more clothing under his coveralls. The mask fit tightly against his face, inducing a sense of claustrophobia, and he could swear that he smelled the damp, sickening odors of the coal dust and the shale/clay bottom rock beneath the mantrip's wheels.

Calm down, he told himself. You're a grown man. You've been underground twice before.

Yeah, but everybody knows the third time is the charm,

taunted another pessimistic voice inside his head. As if in agreement, the mine floor grew rougher, bouncing Steve's head into the scoop's hard steel bed.

Focus on the sound of the rubber wheels whining on the mine floor, he told himself. After a couple of minutes, he felt secure enough to roll over onto his back. His miners lamp shined on the ceiling, and he watched the mine entry's smooth top go zipping by over his head. Only about a foot of distance lay between his face and the rock above.

He brought his wrists slowly across his stomach and chest and crooked his neck to look at his watch.

Ten minutes.

An eternity.

Could he make it though this ordeal without having a nervous breakdown? The last thing these three men needed was the weight of another body to tow out from under the mountain.

He stared at the ceiling. The mantrip passed under a wide crevice in the roof, and a stream of water doused the men.

"Shit," Steve said. The fresh water mixed with the coal dust that had settled on his face mask from the mine floor, and formed little specks of mud that made it almost impossible to see.

Steve heard Elmer's laughter booming under the face mask. "What's a matter, Steve? A little water won't hurt you!"

Steve saw nothing to laugh about; he wiped the mask with his dusty palm, making smears, but at least he could see a little better. He closed his eyes, and imagined that the light reflecting from the roof was the sun coming down upon his closed eyes while he sat reclined in a lawn chair in his front yard.

Unexpectedly, the scoop came to a halt. Steven glanced

at his watch. Twenty minutes since they'd entered the darkness. "What's happened?" he said.

"We've got a lot of rock down across most of the entry," Ron said. "Looks like we're going to have to crawl the rest of the way."

"How far in are we?" Glen asked.

"I'd guess about a mile," Elmer said.

Glen removed a hand held chemical gas detection unit from his bag and held it out in front of him. "The reading is high for methane."

"And there's very little oxygen back in here, so we don't want to overstay our respirators' air supply," Steve said. "I don't want to cut it close. If we don't find them in the next twenty minutes, we'll turn back around and try again tomorrow after we've gotten some of this debris moved out of here."

He crawled close to the left rib, where the roof fall materials were the shallowest, and with his belly and head both scraping rock, he squeezed through. The other three men followed close behind.

They passed beyond the roof fall, and the mine floor was clear once again, but to Steve's disgust, they had entered a water-filled area. At least eight inches of cold water lined the mine floor. Steve felt the water squish between his knee pads and coveralls. For a second, his pace slowed. "Damn, if this don't add insult to injury," he mumbled just loud enough for Elmer, crawling alongside, to hear.

"This ain't nothing, Steve. I've had to work in it for 12 hours with it asshole deep. Don't pay it no mind. It'll get shallower as we near the face, which shouldn't be too long now."

Couldn't come soon enough for me, Steve thought. He struggled to ignore a new, nagging fear that the mine would become inundated with water.

Seventeen minutes after leaving the mine scoop behind, Elmer, who had pushed ahead, said, "I see something up ahead."

The other men joined him, and within a moment, the four approached three chalk covered figures resting within a few feet of the mine face. Steve crawled past the others and knelled over the two smaller figures.

"This is them," he said. "Little Brian and his sister, Jessica."

"What about this man over here?" Ron said. "Could this be old man Elliott? He's been missing for a year and a half, ever since his car was found on top of Bearwallow Mountain."

"That's him," Elmer said. "He used to work with me in the mines, back before he started hitting the bottle regular."

The presence of James Elliott's body indicated to Steve that the previous emergents, those using the host bodies of James and Mona Evans, had first burrowed through the mine seal and used the abandoned mine to store the human 'incubator' of their egg. The bodies of the Evans emergents had not been found, but Steve suspected their remains were somewhere here in the mine.

"But what's this moldy looking stuff all over their skin?" Glen said. "They don't look dead; it's as if they're just napping."

Steve remembered what Donna had said about the possibility that the human skin would undergo some sort of slow transformation as the alien eggs metamorphosed their hosts' internal organs, bones, and fluids beyond recognition.

All the previous emergents had completed their transformation about a year after the burial of the remains of their human hosts, but here was the town drunk, still looking very much the human he had been when he had disappeared nearly 18 months before.

Was there something different about James Elliott's metabolism—perhaps a high blood alcohol content at the time he had been stung by the female emergent—that had delayed or prohibited the transformation process? Or would the hosts who had been implanted with the alien eggs take longer to metamorphose than the human hosts who had ingested the eggs by eating the trout caught from Big Tumbling Creek?

Steve's mining co-worker, Willie Showalter, had been dead for as long as James Elliott had been missing. A couple of months after Willie had been sent to USAMRIID, a sealed coffin said to contain his remains had been returned to his family for burial. Government officials had told his family he had succumbed to a rare form of flesh eating bacteria while being treated for multiple bee stings in a veteran's hospital.

Despite Alan's insistence that it was Willie's body which had been returned, Steve had always doubted. He knew the cover story told to the family was a lie; Donna had said the body was being monitored and analyzed, but she had been reassigned from the evaluation team soon after Willie was shipped to USAMRIID.

Had the body of Willie Showalter completed its transformation in a government laboratory, or had government military scientists found a way to accelerate, decelerate, or suspend the transformation process?

Steve visualized an army of government issued emergents behind enemy lines, and the thought sent a chill through him. He glanced nervously around the immediate area. The ribs on both sides of the entry were relatively clear of debris. The mine floor and top were smooth, no apparent hiding places for anything to be lurking.

He looked again at the white figures lying on the mine floor.

"Maybe they aren't really dead," Ron said. He kneeled over the little girl and placed his head over her chest to listen for a heartbeat.

Everyone seemed to hold their breath as he listened for signs of life. A low, buzzing sound emerged from the silence behind them. They turned, as one, to look back, and it was upon them. Ron, still crouched over Jessica's lifeless body, was hurled with a devastating impact against the mine face, nearly ten feet away.

# CHAPTER 31

Agent Alan Smith paced back and forth before the mine entrance, continually looking at his watch. His brother and the three other men had been underground for thirty-five minutes. By now, they should be near the face—unless something had happened. In an abandoned mine, the risks were huge for a roof fall. The slightest vibration could send tons of roof rock crashing down. If one or more of them should become trapped or injured, it would be impossible to get a second rescue crew in before their air supplies would run out. There was nothing he could do but wait and hope—

The cell phone in the pocket of his suit coat rang.

"Yeah, what do you want?"

"Alan? This is Dr. McKenzie at USAMRIID."

"Have you had a chance to look at the female carcass I had dropped by earlier today?"

"Yes, briefly. I need to see you, right away, about our live specimen."

"I'm afraid it'll have to wait."

"Like hell it will. Do you know what's going on up here?"

"No, and I'm not in any mood for you to tell me." Alan stooped to stare into the dark mine entrance.

"Alan, they've replaced me as head of the team studying the new arrival. A Major Stidham locked a prisoner in the containment cell with the emergent. They murdered the poor man to see how the emergent would react."

"They murdered him, or the thing did?"

"It did. It grabbed him and stung him in the back. Then, they refused to try to get the man out."

"What do you mean, stung him? That was a male we sent you."

"On the outside, yes. But internally, the thing is a female. It has a stinger inside the base of its spine."

"What about the dead female, Tammy, that I brought in today?" His mind raced with the implications. "Was it a male? I mean, we would've noticed male organs, for God's sake."

"Not unless you searched inside its rectum—"

"Wait a minute here. The dead female, Tammy, was really a male. The live male in the lab, Roger, is a fertilized female. So you're telling me that Eddie, the male we're missing—"

"Is probably a female as well," Donna said. "That kid, Amanda, did say she saw one of the dead teenage boys fly away with the little boy and girl, right? That was Eddie, the one we're missing. A male emergent wouldn't have been concerned with securing hosts for eggs, and since he probably had already mated, he would not have had need of the children for their blood. He would have already had his fill of cow's blood, topped off with sex with a female. Lethargy and death were all such a male would have had left to look forward to, but the female would have been guided with purpose, a need for hosts within which to implant her—"

"God, no!"

"What is it, Alan?"

"I'm standing outside an abandoned underground mine site. We think those kids were taken inside. Steve and three other men are back under there trying to recover the kids' bodies."

"You've got to get them out of there. We don't know how long the females live after injecting their eggs, but this one is probably still alive. She'll defend her eggs to the death."

"There's no way to communicate with them. There's absolutely nothing we can do."

"You can go in after them. You've got the prototype with you?"

"Yes, but it's useless. The mine is full of gas. Discharging a weapon in there would bring the whole mountain down on their heads."

"How could you send them into such a place?"

"Look, Donna, roof falls were the most we expected. We counted on what you'd told us. We found what we thought was the dead female at the mouth of the mine. Steve said you told him if the female was dead, it meant the males were already dead."

"How about the one you brought me last night? Did "he" look dead to you?"

"Hey, I'm not the one who said the males die first. Based on what we thought we knew, it appeared that he had already mated. I didn't think it would live through the night. Look, I'm a government agent, not a bug specialist. How was I to know?"

"How were any of us to know? I'm sorry. I knew better than to come to conclusions on such a limited number of samples. I'll be down there on the first flight out."

"There's no need in—" She had hung up. He dropped

the phone back into his jacket and resumed pacing in front of the mine.

# CHAPTER 32

The other three men looked on in stunned disbelief as the naked, grey humanoid insect which had once been teenager Eddie Blevins wrapped its arms and legs about Ron's unconscious body. A long stinger resembling a scorpion's tail flashed out of what had once been the base of the star high school quarterback's spine.

The sharp, hollow pointed stinger plunged firmly into the small of Ron's back and convulsed for a couple of seconds as it administered a paralyzing dose of venom into the young miner's bloodstream. The venom was closely followed by a single, tiny egg that nestled beneath the skin near the victim's spine.

The ovipositor/stinger slowly retracted back into a bump at the base of the spine, then the creature turned its attention and its blazing red eyes to the other men.

"Dear God in Heaven," Glen said. "What have we gotten ourselves into?"

Steve knew; he had trusted too much in Donna's theories. No, not in her theories, but in her initial observations. All the other deceased men and women had metamorphosed into corresponding male and female "emergents." But this male human form housed a female creature, and the vestiges of Eddie Blevins' male organs were as much a useless evolutionary carryover as a human appendix.

What was it Donna once said? Something about insects being fascinating because sometimes none of their body parts are where we expect them to be.

Glen, kneeling to the left of Steve, was hypnotized by the beast, frozen in place.

"Run!" Steve said as the creature lunged along the mine floor toward Glen. As soon as the word left Steve's mouth, the thing was upon the mine inspector. With blinding speed, the grey monster lashed out with the razor like claws of its right hand and loped Glen's head off his body.

The mask-covered head turned somersaults in the air as it flew toward Steve, spraying blood on the clear plastic of his respirator mask as it flew past, narrowly missing him.

Before Glen's head hit the ground, Steve had fled. Had he lingered, he would have seen Elmer pick up a rusty, three-foot length of roof bolt and swing repeatedly at the angry creature. With his back to the left rib of the entry, Elmer swung mightily, cursing, "Bastard" with each blow.

He landed several solid licks on the creature's head and arms, but succeeded in doing nothing more than angering the buzzing hell spawn. After a couple of minutes of non-stop swinging, Elmer's arms grew weaker, his reactions increasingly slower.

The thing seized its opening like a master swordsman. In an instant when Elmer's chest was unprotected, the being jabbed five steel-hard claws into the man's muscular chest. The sternum gave way with a sickening crack, and the daggers pushed like hot knives through butter, becoming stuck for an instant in the coal seam at Elmer's back.

The creature pulled its fist from Elmer's chest, and his lifeless body slumped to the mine floor.

By the time Elmer's valiant struggle had ended, Steve was several hundred yards away from the face. When starting his retreat, he had tried to stand up in the three foot space and banged the upper part of his back soundly into the roof. Now, blood and sweat trickled down his back, but his terror left him oblivious to his injuries.

His heart pounded in his ears so loudly that he stopped hearing the sounds of Elmer's struggles long before his old friend had succumbed. He struggled to see through the blood splattered respirator mask, but dared not pause long enough to bring his hand up to wipe the blood away. Several times, when he had looked away from a small, clear spot in the visor, he banged into the right side of the rib, but he stayed close to that side of the entry.

To the opposite side lay dozens of small, crosscut rooms. In his half-blinded state, it would be so easy to accidentally run repeatedly into one of these shallow chambers and waste precious time trying to find his way out again. It was in one of these shallow crosscuts that the creature had lain in wait, and Steve's haste to reach the face had distracted him from even considering the danger that might lurk within. Of course, even if they had spotted the creature earlier, what difference would it have made?

He strained to listen for the creature's angry buzz above the sound of his own pounding heart, but gave up in light of the futility of it all. He knew what he was up against. Donna said these things could detect the slightest amount of human pheromones from miles away on a windy day, and trace the heat of a human body minutes after it had passed an outdoor space.

If the creature wanted him, it would have him, and since he was still alive, it must still be occupied with the bodies of his friends.

He scrambled onward through the dark stillness, then felt the soothing splash of cold water as he returned to the low point of elevation in the mine floor.

The area of the old roof fall should be coming up soon. He crowded tight against the right rib, and momentarily, his bare hands plowed into the sharp shale that lined the bottom of the narrow hole he and the others had squirmed through minutes earlier. As he twisted and jerked through the hole, his left knee pad fell off, and a shard of shale sliced through his coveralls and into his kneecap.

He felt the knee grow warm with wet blood, but was oblivious to the pain. Just another trail of blood for the land shark. He laughed out loud at the thought of the old Saturday Night Live skit. "Candy gram—Land shark," he said, never slowing his exit.

At last, he plopped through the hole and trained his head lamp on the sweet sight of the mine scoop. He took the time now to drag his wet shirt sleeve across his face mask, and cleared away most of Glen's blood, but his vision was still somewhat obscured by the steam and sweat that had collected inside the mask.

He climbed into the operator's slot in the scoop, and for the first time in his life, cranked the starter of a piece of underground mining equipment. To his delight, the battery powered motor fired right up, and the scoop's four halogen lamps, two front and two rear, flickered into full luminance.

He slammed the scoop into reverse, keeping as tight as possible to the left rib, and occasionally ramming the left front and left rear of the vehicle solidly into the wall as he struggled to get the hang of driving the squat little vehicle. It was hard to drive the vehicle in reverse, but he was afraid to waste the precious seconds it would take to turn the scoop around in one of the crosscut rooms.

He pushed the scoop to its limits, all the while listening for any sounds that might be heard over the whine of the tires on the mine floor. He heard nothing, and as the minutes passed, he allowed himself to hope he would survive this hellish nightmare.

Elmer had estimated the scoop had taken them about a mile into the mine before they encountered the roof fall. Steve could not glance down at his watch, but he guessed he had traveled at least halfway back to the outside.

With any luck, the air in his respirator and the batteries in the scoop would hold out, and the creature would be content with the victims it had already claimed. But if it were coming for him, it would have to crawl, just as he had crawled; the low mine ceiling would make it impossible for the creature to extend its wings and fly after him.

The scoop's open-topped front cab, nearly a foot taller than the rear of the vehicle, would afford a measure of protection by allowing the creature less than a foot of crawl space between the cab and the mine roof.

By keeping the scoop tight against the left rib, that side was protected, but his entire right side would be exposed. An open distance of more than 10 feet lay between the vehicle's right side and the right rib of the entry. If the creature could outrun the scoop, it would be all over. The vehicle's long, open bed would offer Steve up like a turkey on a platter.

For a moment, he was able to ignore his exposed right flank and concentrate on steering the scoop close to the left rib. Then, in the distance, he could make out a slight buzzing sound. Within seconds, it grew louder and louder, like the buzz of an angry hornet.

Steve raised his head as much as he dared over the top of the cab, and about a hundred feet behind the retreating scoop, fixed in his headlights, was the devil with glowing red eyes. Its hind legs and arms dug into the mine floor, with a speed and grace that resembled a greyhound more than anything which had ever been human.

In a worthless gesture, Steve pushed down harder on the throttle, but the batteries were already delivering full power.

The buzzing grew louder, and the blazing eyes grew larger; the thing from who the hell knew where was gaining rapidly on the scoop.

In another instant, it had slammed into the front of the retreating vehicle, but the creature's body lacked sufficient bulk to change the scoop's course. Seconds later, it rammed the cab again, this time shattering the left headlight. Its buzzing grew louder with its frustration.

After two failed attempts to reach its prey, the devil did what Steve had feared; it came around for a run toward his right front end. He looked to the right and found himself staring face to face with the creature's fiery eyes; less than four feet separated Steve from the grim reaper.

He jerked the steering wheel sharply to the right; the scoop's steel side slammed into the creature's right shoulder, throwing it half the distance to the right rib, but not slowing its progress in the least. Again, it crowded close to the scoop, and again, Steve swerved to the right, this time bouncing the angry beast solidly into the right rib.

Seeing his opportunity, Steve veered the scoop toward the rib, pinning the creature against the coal seam and dragging it for nearly twenty feet before it tumbled backward into the next open crosscut.

Steve's hands trembled on the wheel. He did not delude himself into thinking he had inflicted any serious damage on the thing. Its hide was tougher than a rhino's, and there were no bones to break. At best, he had postponed the inevitable for a few more seconds.

A few hundred yards down the entry, he noticed the vehicle's rear lights begin to flicker, and the scoop lost all power and rolled to a stop. The battery power indicator on the control panel showed sufficient charge, but the connectors to the battery had jarred loose, and he had neither the time, nor the knowledge, to implement repairs.

When he crawled out the back of the scoop, the beam from his headlamp caught on something small and metallic at the rear of the bed—it was Elmer's cigarette lighter. Apparently, it had fallen out of his coverall pocket on the ride in. Steve picked it up and clutched it in his right hand as he crawled away from the vehicle. If the bug from hell caught up with him, at least he could deny it the satisfaction of killing him; one flick of the lighter in the dense methane atmosphere would blow them both to kingdom come.

Steve crawled along the mine floor, oblivious to the blood that oozed from his back, knee, and hands. He listened intently for the terrifying buzzing, but the only sounds were the slow drip, drip, drip of water from within the collapsed areas beyond the crosscuts in the next entry, and, of course, the ever-present pounding of his own heart which, he feared, was literally a drum beat that would lead the thing more quickly to him.

Briefly, he sensed a slight increase in temperature, as if he were nearing the outdoors; perhaps its eighty-five degree warmth was making inroads into the cold, damp mine's atmosphere. He squinted to see through the steam rivulets constantly running down the inside of his respirator mask.

If he was close to attaining the outside, there would be some trace of daylight coming down the mine entry's long, dark corridor, but there was no glimmer of light, save for the light of his headlamp. His heart sank for a moment, but his hope returned with a sudden realization.

It was true that the elevation dropped from the face to the outside, but from his days as a mine draftsman, he recalled that changes in elevation were rarely continuous. The mine floor usually made many drastic ups and downs, making it unlikely that a person would ever be able to see the light of the outdoors from very deep in the mine.

Perhaps he truly had felt a current of warm air, and sunlight and salvation might be waiting over the next gradual rise in the mine floor.

Less than five minutes passed before he detected a faint glow ahead. Summoning one last burst of energy, he increased the frantic pace of his crawling. The slope of the mine floor dropped sharply, subjecting his eyes to the blessed sunlight. The light intensity made him squint, but he kept up his desperate pace. No buzz behind him, daylight and life waited a few feet away.

Unexpectedly, a voice just ahead said, "Hit the dirt!"

Steve complied instantly, falling face down upon the coal dust covered mine floor.

There was a sudden flash of light and a deafening boom that seemed to reverberate endlessly down the mine entry. Directly behind him came the horrible dying buzz and death throes of the thing that had unexpectedly stalked him in total silence. The sound of arms and limbs flailing on the mine floor and roof continued for a moment, then stopped.

The creature was dead.

"Come on out, Steve. It hasn't any fight left in it." It was his brother, Alan.

His eyes adjusted to the light; Alan was lying on his stomach less than 20 yards away, wearing night-vision goggles and still holding the shotgun out in front of him. He dropped his weapon and crawled to meet Steve.

"He was right behind me, wasn't he?" Steve said.

"Yes, not more than 10 feet or so."

"What if you'd missed and hit me?"

"I never miss."

"But what if you had?"

"Then I would have wasted my only shot, and been dead, too."

"So you were doubly motivated not to miss." Steve laughed.

Alan pulled off the night-vision goggles. "You might say that, little brother."

"Don't tell me you had birdshot in that 12 gauge."

"A little prototype that Donna and a Pentagon munitions team developed. The cartridge was a diamond-tipped cylinder filled with a super insecticide. Donna said that once the round penetrated the thing's chest, it would release enough anticholinesterase to cause its muscles to spasm, leading to paralyzed breathing, convulsions, and momentarily, death. Apparently, she figured right."

"But she botched up big time on determining the sex of these things," Steve said.

"I know. She discovered her mistake while you guys were underground. There wasn't time to get another respirator or scoop hauled in. I hoped someone would make it close to the outside, and gambled the methane levels would be low enough out here to allow me to fire the shot without blowing up the whole mine."

"Alan, the others—I think they're all dead."

"You're not sure?"

"I saw Ron and Glen die. I left Elmer to fight it alone. I turned tail and ran—"

"No, you did the only sensible thing. If you hadn't made it out, they all would've died in vain."

Steve held out his right hand and unclenched his fist, revealing the cigarette lighter.

"What are you doing with that?"

"It was Elmer's. One last chance for me to finish what he started." Steve stared at the lighter for a second, then dropped it into the breast pocket of his coveralls.

"Let's get out of here, Alan."

# EPILOGUE

By morning, Alan had flown in a federal team to remove the dead creature and its six human victims. Body bags containing the mangled remains of Ron, Glen, and Elmer were sealed at the mine site and flown to USAMRIID for autopsy. Doctors would remove the egg that the creature had injected into Ron, and the other two men would be examined for the presence of eggs.

After the autopsies, their remains would be returned to their families, who would be told that their loved ones had been crushed beyond recognition in a massive roof fall.

Alan promised Steve the bodies of the two children would be returned to their mother for burial as soon as the alien eggs were removed. He made no similar promise about the town drunk's body; James Elliott had no known blood relatives. His fate would remain a mystery to the populace, while, in the coming months, his slowly evolving remains would disclose volumes about the metamorphosis from human to emergent.

Donna had taken an early morning flight, and before noon was ringing Steve's doorbell.

He climbed out of bed, threw on a robe, and opened the door. Donna greeted him with a long, hard kiss. He pulled her inside and pushed the door shut with his foot.

"How are you?" she said.

"Sore as hell, but I'll recover, once I get a decent night's sleep."

"Nightmares?"

"Not exactly. Ever read any Robert Frost?"

"Not that I remember," she said.

"In college, I read his poem 'Apple Picking Time.' The person in the poem talks about picking so many apples all day long that when they finally go to sleep, all they see are apples all over the place in their dreams. With me, last night, it was ants everywhere, crawling around—"

"Over you?"

"No. In front of my face. I was staring down at them, watching them going in and out of their holes in the ground. I used to do that a lot as a kid; Alan got me into it, I guess."

"He mentioned something about you both being little naturalists as boys. Maybe you missed your calling."

"You going back to work for him?"

"After nearly three years on this project, I've had enough of the way the government does things. Besides, I'm always a little antsy—pardon the pun. I have other projects to get back to. My suitcase was packed for Asia when I got called in on this."

"How long will you be gone?"

"A long time. Gonna miss me?"

"More than you can imagine."

"Come to Borneo with me."

"You'd have me?"

"Oh, yeah. You're a fascinating specimen, for a Homo sapiens." She smiled and stared lovingly into his eyes.

"Definitely a subject worthy of further study." She untied his robe and pushed it off his shoulders. He blushed as she softly traced her fingertips around a nasty scrape on his chest.

"Careful." Steve grinned. "I'm a wounded man."

"I promise to be gentle."

That evening, after Donna had doctored his wounds and attended to his needs, Steve slept.

For the first time since childhood, he revisited his most cherished dream, but this time, he was not the future Steve, the twenty-two-year-old of super heroic proportions, rather, he was himself—the man the boy had grown to be.

He floated out the open window of his bedroom, into the clear skies of a summer's night. Weightless, he drifted high over the house, then set his course by the full moon hanging high over the horizon.

He flew over familiar pasture fields, the neighborhood grocery, the car dealership, and the cemetery, before losing his conscious self somewhere between the sky and tall trees bathed in moonlight.

He rejoiced, and his spirit joined with the wind and soared beyond all physical care. Until waking, he flew as unshackled men have flown since the dawn of time— without the wings of angels or the pinions of birds, or the artifice of steel, or wire, or canvas—solely upon the wings of determination, imagination, and desire.

The End

# About the Author

Danny Cantrell is a native of Appalachia. He has had a life-long fascination with insects, and has worked in both the coal mining industry and in higher education. He holds an associate degree in mining engineering technology, the bachelors and masters' degrees in English, and the Ed.D. in leadership studies in higher education administration. He is also the author of the non-fiction book, *The Unwritten Law: A True Crime of Passion*, an account of one of the most divisive murder trials of the Roaring 20s (available in trade paperback and Kindle formats). His hobbies include travel, reading, watching TV dramas, listening to a wide variety of music, and photography. He and his wife, Connie, reside in Cabell County, West Virginia with a Peter Pan dog, three loving cats, and more books and magazines than 10 normal households should contain.

www.ingramcontent.com/pod-product-compliance
Lightning Source LLC
Chambersburg PA
CBHW060432130626
46555CB00005B/2320